The Cornflake House

Deborah Gregory

PICADOR USA
New York

Picador® is a U.S. registered trademark and is used by St. Martin's
Press under license from Pan Books Limited.

For information on Picador USA Reading Group Guides, as well as
ordering, please contact the Trade Marketing department at
St. Martin's Press.
Phone: 1-800-221-7945 extension 763
Fax: 212-677-7456
E-mail: trademarketing@stmartins.com

Library of Congress Cataloging-in-Publication Data

Gregory, Deborah.
    The cornflake house / Deborah Gregory.
        p.   cm.
    ISBN 0-312-20290-3 (hc)
    ISBN 0-312-25271-4 (pbk)
    I. Title
PR6057.R3856C67 1999
823'.914—dc21   99-25324
                                                             CIP

First published in Great Britain by Picador, an imprint of Macmillan
Publishers Ltd.

First Picador USA Edition: May 2000

10 9 8 7 6 5 4 3 2 1

To my mother, Kathleen,
and to the memory of my father, 'Pab'

One

Today for the first time my magic has let me down. No warning that something – sorry, someone – special was about to enter my life. Not one tingle down my usually sensitive spine, nor one buzz in my brain. An intangible beast, magic, but I find myself searching for it now in my cell, as if it were a lost coin. Oh, of course, the warder told me that, once I'd completed my toilet duties, a prison visitor would be waiting for me. I was informed, but not prepared for who I found there. We're allowed to wear a little make-up and stud earrings; had my head or my heart given me even a tiny inkling about you, I would have made roses of my lips and filled my ears with pearls. Instead I'm forced to admit that I looked my worst, and probably smelt of lavatory cleaner.

Perhaps I'm misreading the situation; after all, your unannounced appearance had, for me, all the panache of the old rabbit-from-a-hat trick. Only this time, the trick's on me.

You must be wondering what this is all about; why the fuss? Meeting you, Matthew Pritchard, visitor extraordinaire, was the surprise of my life. I am – an unusual state for somebody with sixth sense – in shock. This means that you must be as special as me. Nobody has ever before taken away my breath and my magic in one instance.

I'm sorry for the earlier lack of communication, sorry I sat there like a tailor's dummy while you tried to get to know me. Now, alone in my cell, I wish I had at least offered you a word or two, so that you'd be hearing my voice as you read this. You mustn't see our meeting as a failure, you did all you could. No one could have been more patient or considerate. I was simply struck dumb. And I especially appreciated the way you didn't pry into my case, although I guess you must have wondered how I came to do, or to be accused of doing, the terrible crime that brought me here. Was my crime the reason you chose me to visit? If so, I'm glad my once-in-a-lifetime act of violence brought me here, to a place where you come and go.

I intend to make up for that lost opportunity, for my sealed lips, by writing this to you. I want you to know me; yes I know that'll seem odd coming from a woman who didn't so much as nod her head in the Visitors' Room, but nothing matters more to me now. Were you allowed to see my file? I'm new to this, my family had its brushes with the law in the past, but we were cautioned, fined or, in the case of my son, given Community Service. Ironically, Community Service was exactly what my boy thought he'd been doing when he committed his offences, but never mind. What I mean is I've never been either prisoner or prison visitor before; I don't know the ropes. But if they've showed you my file, I suppose you'll have done your homework and read my background. You know my age, will understand that the first flush of youth has faded to a pale colour-wash. And then you must have read about The Cornflake House, about

2

my large and shall we say non-conformist family. I wish you could have met them. We'd have laid on tea for you on a Sunday. The neighbours would've watched you, as they watched everybody else, walking up to our house, and they'd have thought how surprisingly normal you looked, considering. Then one of us, Zulema say, in her dress of midnight blue threaded with silver moons, would have opened the door and welcomed you. I'd have been shy as I introduced you to my relations, but Mum would have given you a nip of something special to break the ice. Before long we'd have been laughing and catching each other's eyes as we sampled Mum's baking and suffered my brother Django's insults.

I wish I had a file on you, Matthew. Not just papers telling me your date of birth . . . mind you I do wonder . . . but a thick stack of reading full of details like whether you can see anything at all without those dear, round glasses, what food gives you most pleasure and do you prefer baths to showers? But then, you have only my skeleton in your possession, the bare bones, so until I'm through with my story don't think you have too much of an advantage. I know already, for example, that you are a brave man, one who has come to terms with his lack of height. Even though it meant tilting your head at an angle likely to leave you with pains in the neck, you never stopped looking me straight in the eye. In a narrow-minded world such as ours, you must have suffered for your stature . . . but now you might allow yourself a smile as you read that today you met a woman, a tall, imposing – I like that so much better than the word big – woman who knows all there is to know about prejudice and who finds you irresistible.

Also, you must be an intrepid soul to enter a prison of your own free will. The very word, like cancer, fills the weak-spirited with dread. I know when my son was up before the beak I prayed for him to stay out of gaol. Not only is it hard for a mother to cope with the prospect of her child's confinement, but the thought of visiting him, making that journey into the unknown, made me ill with worry. Luckily, I suppose, when I first came here I was in a haze of sorrow and confusion. I heard the infamous clanking of doors, smelt the mixture of chlorine, urine, mustiness and cabbage, but hardly took any of it in to my muddled brain. They say those who fall are often cushioned by shock, and certainly in my case the worst was absorbed, zapped if you like, by the electrifying horror of what had just happened. I've seen that stunned look on the faces of fellow inmates; you're never alone in prison.

Now, brave visitor, I'm about to ensure that we'll know each other better. Something I was lucky enough to glimpse, to marvel at, as we shook hands, encourages me to believe it will be worth my while. As you reached to take my hand in introduction, I was embarrassed to meet your eyes. I focused instead on your hand and wrist. I saw the shine on your worn but clean white shirt, the fluffy fringe where your cord jacket rubs against the world. And I noticed, to my astonishment and delight, your cute cuff link. Are you blushing, Matthew? I do hope not. Why shouldn't you wear something whimsical? What was it made of? It looked like black enamel, with a tiny red collar, on silver. I saw the pair of them, tail to tail when you pressed all ten of your fingers together. Scottie-dog cuff links, wonderful. Wear them with pride. They're inspirational. I'd have fallen for you anyway, but I'm not sure I'd have found the nerve to write this if you'd held your sleeves together with the usual square or oval objects.

So, my turn now; I am the oldest of seven children; seven was an essential number to Mum. I have two sisters, Zulema and Perdita, and four brothers, Fabian, Merry, Django and Samik – my mum favoured the unusual. I promise you shall meet them properly in time. My mother taught me to introduce myself by saying, 'I am Eve, the first born.'

She liked us to take the wind out of people's sails from the first moment, she thrived on giving surprises, my mother. I assume this was because, being clairvoyant, she was rarely taken aback herself. I inherited my magic from her; she was the centre of my universe. Obviously my records will tell of her recent death, of her dramatic and, to some minds, grisly departure from this world. But do they even hint at the grief this death has caused? Well no, how could they? Why should they? It has nothing, officially, to do with my case. Even my family can have no idea how I suffered, am still suffering. Loss; I could write of chasms, of black holes where once there was so much colour, but I would never touch the truth of it. This may sound ridiculous, coming from a daughter, but I had no life without Mum; there's no part of my history which isn't centred on her. I never broke away, as most adults do. I made a few pathetic attempts to leave home, to travel, to fall in love. But The Cornflake House was a powerful magnet, or perhaps I should say it was a comforting roost. I was always the homing pigeon, back before darkness fell.

Magic and death; there is a link the human mind can't

handle. In my case, death has caused a halt to magic. For my mother it was the other way around; magic brought about her death.

It wasn't only the magic that made her special. Her warm lap or wide arms were always ready to accommodate a tearful, wounded child. She was seldom cross or critical, as other mothers were. Our achievements met with instantaneous praise and a spontaneous, joyful hug, but her expectations of us never soared to the unattainable. To her we seven were a species apart, élite, infallible. It was wonderful to be amongst the select, perhaps especially enchanting to be the eldest of the tribe, chosen one of the chosen. I grew up with a deep sense of my own importance within my family and within the world.

I imagine everybody feels partly as I do when their mother dies, unsheltered, as if a wrap of finest feathers, not wings but a cloak they never previously appreciated, has been spirited from their bodies. Left standing, bewildered, without the one person who loved us unconditionally, uncritically. Without the one who made us who we are. Ordinary, with the harsh, disapproving population of planet earth to please all of a sudden.

I do understand how curious you must be about my recent past, but I feel happier, safer, beginning with my mother's story. What frightens me is the way control has taken over from chaos. I like chaos; it's what I'm used to. Prison life leaves no room for muddle; somehow I've lost my identity in all this routine. I need to talk about the distant past before we get to the present.

My mother always maintained that she was sold to her parents by the Gypsies. If this was nothing more than a childhood fantasy, she never outgrew it. She did possess many of the attributes we usually associate with Romanies, a love of the outdoors, the gift of telling fortunes. Besides, my granny, Editha, who lived with us for the last years of her life, never refuted this claim. Granny used to smile and nod at the story, even adding details of her own to embellish it, although these personal touches changed with each telling. The idea that my grandparents had paid a sum of their hard earnt cash for my mother had a faint ring of truth to it, because they'd been childless for years beforehand. Then there was the way my mother looked, which wasn't remotely like either parent. She was brown the year round, tanned even in places which were never exposed to the sun, whereas Editha, like me, was golden haired with pink and white skin. Eric, my grandad, was bald by the time I came along, but you could see from his freckled arms and bushy eyebrows that he'd been a roaring red-head in his day. He was an ugly bugger, physically and mentally. Women who met my grandad didn't fancy shaking hands with him, let alone getting into his bed. Maybe Editha went along with the Gypsy story to deflect people from considering another possibility. Well, if she did spend a blissful moment or two in the arms of a dark stranger in order to conceive, few would have blamed her for it.

It took one of history's worst storms to make my mother feel proud to call herself Editha's daughter. By then the Gypsy story was too deep rooted to be discarded, and so she let it stay and stay. For my generation it was a family legend, and we children were eager to believe it. Apart from the glamour, the romance of being one quarter Gypsy, we clung to this possible heritage as a safeguard against the taunts of schoolmates. It made us stronger, when strength was needed in a hostile playground, the chance that Gypsy blood flowed through our heated veins. We weren't invincible in battle, but when we fell our enemies were seldom rewarded with the sight of a Cornflake House kid in tears. I know that I for one carried another child inside my soft, blonde self, a dark, bright girl who was light on her feet, swift with her tongue and whose heart was the colour and texture of a walnut. I would never let her down.

Also, there was the question of our relations. We loved Granny Editha well enough, in spite of her irritating little ways, but none of us would have chosen to believe we were related to Eric. He frightened and fascinated us. Much as we all yearned to have a man in our lives, we fled from his company. At least he couldn't chase after us; part of his menace lay in the fact that he had only one leg.

Before my grandmother met Eric she ran her fenland smallholding on her own. When her parents died, she carried on picking fruit, feeding chickens and hoeing the vegetable patch in all the fierce variety of weather. How was she to know, as she accepted the offer of marriage from the knife and scissors sharpener who called on her one day, then came back and called again the next, that she would still be running the place on her own after her wedding? Having hardly ever ventured away from her square, flat homestead, having met so few people before, I suppose Editha thought she'd done well for herself by marrying at all. I once overheard my mother asking Grandma why she'd hitched up with Eric, and the answer was 'because he came, it seemed meant – once he was on the doorstep'. There you have it, as simple a truth as the answer, 'because he asked me,' which must have been given by a million spouses. Editha wasn't young, had no expectations, and Eric can't have been so dreadful at that time when he had both his legs, all his hair and a flat stomach as yet unstuffed with Grandma's chickens and potatoes.

What you also have, in that answer of Editha's, is the seed of one of the ruling factors in my own mother's life. She believed implicitly in certain things being meant to be. Who knows how different our lives would've been if that belief hadn't existed? We would never have been brought up in The Cornflake House without it; maybe never have been born at all.

Whatever else he did – or mostly didn't – do, Eric has to be given credit for loving his baby girl. In that, at least, Editha was always able to defend him. He might have been the fattest, laziest slob who ever sat by a fire day in, day out, but he doted on the brown-haired, brown-eyed baby. Not that fatherhood inspired him to get off his backside and make more money, his grinding wheel lay rusting in an outhouse right through his daughter's childhood, but he was generous with his smiles. He must have loved to see his little girl running around, helping her mother to keep the place going. By the time she was four my mother was capable of dragging a full scuttle of coal from shed to kitchen. According to Mum, she was six when her dad taught her how to chop wood, small pieces at first, of course; Editha tackled the full sized logs.

Then it was time for Eric's little helper to get an education. She walked the mile or so to school alone, her route a dead straight line across the wetlands, following a ditch between raised fields. I've walked that journey with her, a nostalgia trip, and I know how exposed to the winds and the rains she was. What strikes you is the absence of landscape and colour; an artist, especially in winter, would need only to mix greys and dull greens to do justice to that scene. Whichever way you turn, the horizon is spiked with church spires, but no other landmarks are visible. The only trees there are willows which grow along the steep bank. These have been cropped by the locals and stunted by gales until their trunks are dwarfish, their branches skeletal. There was little comfort at the end of Mum's journey either. Like most buildings in the area, the school was a makeshift affair. We looked for it together, Mum and I. After all the stories, I was excited at the prospect of seeing the buildings; but they'd disappeared. New houses stood on the site, their gardens covering the old playground. This is probably no bad thing for my mother's generation, some pretty horrific memories were attached to the place.

Before its demise, the school consisted of one central brick hall surrounded by 'temporary' wooden classrooms with tin roofs. On wet days the rain played these roofs like steel bands and old stoves, which smoked at the teacher's end of the classrooms, were encircled by small pairs of steaming boots and shoes.

It's difficult to picture my unconventional mother as a schoolgirl, but schoolgirl she was. A dark, secret creature, decidedly unkempt, dirty even. Her toes, inside worn sandals, seemed to have been outlined by thick pencil, and her heels were hard as earth in a drought. Her bare legs were tanned all year round and her once green dress had been washed until it was a thin, sad yellow. Around her oval face she wore her hair, which was almost black and hung in natural ringlets, cropped to fall on a level with her lips. Ribbons, slides, hairgrips, she hated all of these. When the ringlets reached her chin she chopped them off herself.

She told us how her class teacher, a washed-out creature called Miss Downy, hated her. Apart from her untidy appearance, my mother had an unusual, perhaps rather silly name. She was called Victory. This wasn't short for Victoria, as many supposed it to be, but was actually another extension of Victor. The Victor she was named after had been, apparently, a bit of a lad and much admired by Eric who was his closest friend.

Victor had died on a train, or rather off a train which had been speeding from London to Peterborough. Both Eric and Victor had been full of drink and bravado on that fateful journey, showing off for the benefit of two unfortunate young women who had no choice but to share a carriage with these loudmouths. Hiccupping into the face of the girl he preferred, Victor had boasted how fast he was in all things.

'No stopping me, is there Eric?' he slurred. No doubt Eric had nodded loyally.

'Well, you'll have to stop at Huntingdon,' the young woman quipped, 'we all will.'

Determined not to be stumped, Victor had told her he could get to Peterborough faster by road.

'Oh yes?'

'Yes.'

It was the last word he was to utter. Well, he may have cursed as he hit the ground, but there was nobody with him to record the fact. Eric's eyes would moisten as he told of the rush of wind which swept through the carriage when Victor opened the door . . .

'He was one of the best,' he'd assure us, shaking his huge head. Then a smile would cross Eric's face and he'd nod knowingly. 'Still, he was right after all. Train hit a stray cow, stopped for hours while they cleared the line. Police car picked up Victor's body, drove him to Peterborough and there he was, when we pulled in, waiting for somebody to identify him.'

Editha would whisper to us children that the end of this story was pure fiction, sugar to sweeten a bitter pill, and we believed her. But since invention wasn't one of Eric's strong points, we grew up confused, yet with the whole scene in our heads: the corpse in the police car was always pictured smiling, grinning even, having had the last laugh.

There was never any question of a second child. Eric named his only offspring after his only friend. I expect the 'y' was Editha's contribution. Victory had no second name.

Of course Victory's teacher didn't dislike her merely because of her name and her dishevelment. She could have been a filthy child called Battle Zone and been teacher's pet if only she'd behaved herself. But Victory wasn't an ideal girl to have in a class of reasonably well-behaved between the wars children. For a start she abhorred rules and regulations, or at least found them wholly incomprehensible. Why must a drawing be the size of one small piece of paper? Why should a poem have more than two lines but less than twenty? Why all sit together, stand in rows, walk in crocodiles and eat the same food? It made no sense to that one little girl.

War was waged between the difficult child and the uncompromising Miss Downy. The teacher had her own armoury, of course; the ruler and the weight of authority. But Victory had a secret, superior weapon which she could use without moving from her desk or batting an eyelid. In fact batting an eyelid would have ruined everything, because the secret weapon was The Stare. The trick was to stare for some time and with unwavering concentration at an object, until said object responded in its way. It was as simple as that.

The Stare could cause sticks of chalk to snap in two just as Miss Downy began to write on the blackboard. Under pressure from The Stare, the heel of one of the unfortunate teacher's shoes was seen to tremble and collapse. A chair leg fell off, landing Miss Downy on the floor. The door refused to open when class was over; and, my mother's personal favourite, one beautifully straight-seamed stocking succumbed to the pull of The Stare and burst with a joyful ping from the grip of Miss Downy's suspenders.

Miss Downy was, naturally, suspicious; but who in their right mind would accuse a small girl of such trickery? Although she couldn't blame Victory outright, the teacher subjected her to punishments both physical and mental. She found fault with all of Victory's work, often holding up pages of writing for the entire class to ridicule. This left my poor mother with a lifelong complex about reading and writing; she would do neither in front of anybody else – although I often came across her struggling with a letter or a book when she thought she was alone.

For hours at a time the other children saw only the back of the scruffy child as she stood in a corner or faced the blackboard. Victory's classmates were perfectly content to laugh out loud at her when they were all assembled under Miss Downy's supervision, but they gave her a wide berth in the playground or when passing in corridors. They knew instinctively that she was too frightening a soul for them to bully, and too dangerous for them to befriend.

The pupil–teacher war reached a climax one day in January, in the so-called spring term. During the morning lessons Victory began to shake violently. At first she couldn't explain herself to the angry Miss Downy, but when pressed she muttered that it was the roof which was frightening her. Encouraged by their teacher's sneer, the whole class tittered. All eyes peered upwards at the ceiling which looked exactly as it always did. More giggles followed, until order was called.

'I've had just about enough of this silliness,' Miss Downy complained, as if Victory was forever finding fault with parts of the building. 'You will sit still on your seat or you can stand in the corner until break-time.'

Without further invitation, Victory scraped back her chair and hurried to her usual corner.

I'm sorry Matthew. We'll have to leave young Victory there, facing the wall, for a while. My cell mate has returned from the laundry, her face puce, her hands wrinkled from steam and hot water. Her return means lunch is nearly ready and hungry or not, when the bell tolls . . .

I share this little home from home with a lass called Liz who's as dark as I am fair but otherwise similar to me in that she chooses silence instead of chatter. On my first day, using a language of grunts and nods, we laid down a few ground rules; as long as we stick to these I see no reason for the quiet, but not antagonistic, status quo to change. I shall return to rescue Mum from her corner when I have stuffed myself with whatever delicacies the kitchen staff have dreamt up for our delight.

Two

Rice pudding; one of the few foods which manages to be disgusting and comforting. I would describe the main course, but even after my efforts I doubt if you'd be any the wiser. Besides, why should you share my abundant interest in food? I can't imagine that you were also brought up in a clutter of children, that you know what it is to have to fight for every slice of bread, to dash for the last biscuit, to wonder how it feels to own a whole packet of crisps. I bought myself some Kraft Cheese Slices with my first wages, sat in a secret place near home and scoffed the lot. I remember the luxury of having so much, the completeness of those squares as I folded them, not to be divided amongst my siblings, but in order to fit an entire slice into my greedy mouth.

Liz is asleep above me. She was reading, but now I can hear that tell-tale breathing which is almost a snore. I find the routine of prison life infuriating, Liz finds it exhausting. I feel like a schoolgirl, sneaking out to meet a forbidden boy. These bunks creak, but I'll brave it. I need to sit at the desk to write properly.

I'll take you back to that different time and place, to the East of England whose flatlands have a temporary air, as if a wave might come and reclaim them any moment. To the company of an unusual little girl who stands in a corner of her classroom because she says she's afraid of the roof. In this child's company, anything is possible; but right now she's just a vulnerable schoolgirl, shivering, close to tears of fear and frustration.

In vain the class tried to ignore the virtual rattling of the child in the corner as the minutes to break-time crawled by. Finally the bell rang and they all escaped to the freezing playground.

'The sky was just a white sheet,' my mother would say when telling this tale, 'as still as a shroud on a corpse. And so it stayed, right through break and on into the next lesson, which was, as I remember, arithmetic. I was so scared I couldn't speak, not that anyone would have listened to my warning. I went straight back to my corner without being told. I felt it was safest. The children were doing sums, heads down over their books, and Miss Downy was marking homework. How they managed not to notice the silence I shall never understand. It was as if the world was holding its breath and all the animals had gone underground, the birds too.'

It was a freak storm; everybody who discussed it afterwards used that word, freak. It came from nowhere and hurled the still English countryside into sudden, devastating turmoil. Throughout the little school doors slammed and window panes cracked in two. The wind rushed through the cloakroom and ripped all the coats from their pegs. Gym bags were tossed about like kites and a flood of rainwater appeared instantly in every doorway. In the playground swings wound themselves round and round their frames, while the one and only tree creaked, swayed and shed branches like tears. But while the rest of the school was being amazed by such trifles, Victory's class were hanging on to their desks for dear life, because they were actually exposed to the battling elements by the sudden disappearance of their roof.

With wonderful ease, the preternatural wind plucked the tin roof from the classroom and left the children screaming at the dreadful sky. Within seconds they were soaked through and frozen. In sheer panic they clutched each other and the furniture. Arithmetic books flew like birds above their heads. The little girls' skirts blew skywards and their plaited hair whipped their faces. Hysteria spread from child to child.

'Down on the floor,' screamed Miss Downy as the roof, a silver, headless pterodactyl, flapped away from sight. The wind ate the teacher's words. The children stampeded, charging through the door, fighting their way to the playground following the flight of their roof.

'It was *War Of The Worlds*, played out for us right there in our own familiar yard,' my mother said. 'The black sky ripped by lightning flashes, wind so strong it was lifting us off our feet and bringing objects from miles away to display before it jerked them on again, dustbin lids, pots, even a whole washing line complete with mangled, twisted laundry. And the roof, so unwieldy and threatening as it hung over us, but wonderful too, awesome and alien being freed like that from all its confines.'

The children were gathered up, herded back into the comparative safety of the brick-built hall where they found the rest of the school sitting in a clutch on the floor.

'It was then that I began to feel the pain,' Victory

explained to us, her children. 'At first I ached all over, but looking around me I could see others were scratched and shaken so I supposed I'd bumped into something when running from my classroom. Those of us who'd been outside were frozen, the sound of teeth rattling was a kind of harmony to the awful noises coming from the weather itself. I tried to concentrate on them, the sounds, but the pain was too strong and then I realized it wasn't all over me anymore, it was only in my right leg. In my right thigh. It was so sharp I wanted to cry out, but I bit my tongue. I must have gone a funny colour, I caught Miss Downy giving me a worried look, probably thinking "whatever next". Then she turned away and I took a peep at my thigh, lifting my frock to see if perhaps my knicker elastic was too tight, praying that I'd find a wound which would take away the feeling of dread. But there was nothing, not a mark on me.'

The whole school sat shivering and listening. Amongst the howling of the wind and crashing of thunder there was one almighty thump which shook the building. Then, as quickly as it had arrived, the storm left them and went to cause havoc somewhere else.

'I didn't find the passing of the storm as comforting as most,' my mother told us, 'because I was sure the pain, which now felt like a saw cutting through me, meant there was worse to come.'

The Headmaster stood on the platform and spoke to his quivering flock.

'We have had a bad storm, a freak storm,' he told them, as if they didn't know, 'but now it has passed and we must all try to calm ourselves, to carry on as normal. In a few minutes it will be dinner time, and I would like my class to get the tables and benches set up, please. A hot meal will do us the world of good. The rest of you can stay in here, but move to the sides please.' For a few minutes the ploy worked, children forgot their fear as they shifted to the sides of the hall or pulled out the furniture for dinner. Many hands were raised because many small bladders could contain themselves no longer, but the Head told them to wait until he had a chance to check the playground. The toilets were outside.

It was at this point in the story that we, Victory's children, would snuggle down in bed, pulling our covers up for protection. For once we'd be glad we had to share our bedrooms. Knowing what came next only made the tale more gruesome. We trembled as we anticipated the arrival of the Roof Giant.

Once everything was ready for dinner there was quiet in the hall, and not a sound from outside.

'Then my leg gave way under me,' Mum would say, 'and I collapsed on the floor, unable to get up. All eyes turned on me, but only for a second because that was when the sound came. It was the sound of a giant climbing out of bed, his bones creaking as he lifted one leg, "Errrumpth," then the other, "Grraahh." And it came from directly over our heads. We hardly had time to wonder what it was when an almighty crash was heard, and hurrying to the windows the braver kids called, "It's fallen, it's in the playground." '

It seems that for a short time there'd been two roofs over the school hall; the freed tin roof had landed there, balancing precariously on top of the tiled one. Then it had shifted, the Roof Giant as we called it, and tumbled to earth. This time not even the Headmaster could control the children. The entire school ran outside, eager to explore this tunnel in the playground.

'There was such a din,' my mother would whisper as we lay in our beds, 'boys whooping, girls yelling, children kicking the roof and running sticks along it to make it echo and sing. It looked as if there should be a house underneath it, buried in the concrete. It was inviting and uninviting all at the same time, but it had to be explored. Not by me, I was still dragging my right leg along, wincing as the pain increased. I made it to the cloakroom door, but no further. I was still convinced there was something bad, something worse than the roof, to come, but those few moments when the other children first broke away to go exploring were pure delight for them.'

Of course it was dark in the roof-tunnel, the far end was resting against a classroom, so light could only get in the near end. The first adventurers to brave going inside screamed as they bumped into each other and tripped each other up. Their cries had the hollow distant sound of riders in a ghost train, thrilling and chilling the timid outsiders. Amongst all this noise, my mum picked out the genuine, piercing screams of a little girl called Kathleen Tucker.

'She's found him, she's found him,' my mother shouted. And this time Miss Downy, who was standing just behind the semi-collapsed child, acted. She grabbed the school bell and churned it up and down until it rang louder than ever before.

'Get back inside,' she ordered between clangs, 'all of you, this instant, back inside.'

Victory pressed herself to the wall as a few obedient children reluctantly passed by. Then Miss Downy went to the mouth of the roof-tunnel and rang her bell there, making a dreadful echoing knoll to which all but one adventurer responded by coming out holding their ears. When the teacher laid the bell on the ground there was only one sound left, the clear high screams of Kathleen Tucker who had reached the point where nothing short of a slap would calm her.

'She had only found his leg,' my mother explained, his right leg, the only part of Donald Clark which was actually in the roof-tunnel. Poor Kathleen had stumbled on this limb and, thinking it was part of a teasing playmate, had tried to kick it out of her way. But it was stuck fast, a fact she realized when she felt around in the near darkness and discovered there was no body, no second leg or trunk, attached to it. Although she was shocked by the leg and the state Kathleen was in, Miss Downy did the right things. She led the trembling child from the tunnel and gave her into the care of another teacher. She couldn't find the words to answer questions, to say what it was that had upset Kathleen so, but she squeezed her way down the outside of the roof-tunnel and came across the rest of Donald wedged there.

The Headmaster called for the ambulance and the fire brigade, there was some heavy lifting to be done. Donald was freed from his tin prison and taken to hospital. His classmates suffered more from the trauma than he did, initially. He was, thankfully, unconscious when found. As they carried him on his stretcher across the playground his almost severed leg refused to join the remainder of his body, it simply wouldn't lie parallel but dangled at an aberrant angle from under the grey blanket.

It was this sight that woke the children of my mother's school in the nights that followed, this glimpse of the abnormal sent their fingers creeping under the covers, feeling for reassurance. It kept us, the next generation awake, for long hours too, but we were always ready to hear the story again and again.

The teachers, who tried not to mention the storm too often in the company of their pupils, spoke of little else in the staffroom, and they discovered that many of the children had taken to absent-mindedly rubbing the tops of their right thighs in class. As if they, like Victory, were suffering in sympathy with Donald who had, ultimately, lost his right leg and who then lay recovering in hospital.

'Donald had always had a problem with his bowels, they didn't work to order,' Mum told us, 'so although he tried to start and finish what he had to do during break-time, he was often still there, sitting in one of the outside toilets, when the bell rang. He got caught by the storm, stranded on the far side of safety. They found the door of the toilet he'd used hanging by one hinge, whether he'd kicked it in an attempt to get somebody to rescue him – his shouts would never have been heard above the roaring wind – or whether the storm had tried to invade, was never clear. He became a hero overnight, and he'd been a quiet, unassuming little boy 'til then. But once he was back with us we bestowed on him instant charisma, or perhaps his limp and his false leg did that for him. Nothing was more provoking and exciting than to get Donald to tell of how he'd sat, trapped on his throne as the world outside his door churned. How he'd waited and waited and, best of all, seen the Roof Giant land on the hall, watched it coming to rest. Then, once the storm was over and everything seemed calm, how he'd stood up, looked around and decided to make a dash for it. But his tummy hurt him, he clung to the wall and had to take one slow step at a time. He'd heard the roof before he saw it, being doubled up with pain. Then . . .

'Well, we tried to help him out, but the poor lad couldn't remember anything else, so the less thoughtful children used to fill in the gaps for him. He was never allowed the luxury of pretending it hadn't happened.'

My mother's pain stopped the moment the authorities took over. Her own leg was cured as she walked back home. We wondered if it was a sort of double premonition she had, if she'd felt so deeply for Donald because of a subconscious knowledge of what was to come for her own father. Eric's condition fascinated and frightened us but we were never able to make Victory speak of it with any emotion other than scorn. She told us that neither her mind nor her body would have felt sympathy for Eric because he deserved none. There were those, and my mother said this as if she was numbered amongst them, who said they wouldn't put it past Eric to have chopped off his own leg so as not to have to work at all, ever again. Of course this was rubbish; he was hardly working himself to the bone before it happened.

Mind you, in a way he did chop off his own leg, or made a good start to the job. It happened before I was born, one day when Editha was down with a bad dose of flu, far too poorly to carry let alone to chop wood. Grumbling all the way to the wood shed, Eric grudgingly picked up a log, set it too close to the edge of the chopping block and raised the axe. The log shot into the air as the axe came down and Eric, slipping backwards, made an impressive and very bloody dent in his left leg, about halfway between knee and ankle. They had no telephone, besides, Eric, not being a great one for doctors, wouldn't have phoned for help anyway. Instead he limped to the house, called Editha from her sick bed, made such a fuss that she was barely able to clean the wound, then sat for several weeks without letting her change his bandage. Did he not want the leg to heal? We shall never know; only Victory ever had the courage to ask and he gave her a gruesome snarl in answer. As Eric's luck would have it, Editha recovered and was well enough to walk out for help not long after gangrene set in. It was also fortunate for our grandfather that the day they came and carted him off for his amputation, was the very day Chamberlain made his 'no such undertaking' speech; so Eric was able, by a hair's breadth, to boast that he'd lost his leg in the war.

Being an amputee sets one apart, it must be like being blond in China. Although we were a hotchpotch of children and often stared at for our own differences, we were as prone to gaze and gawp at Grandad as any stranger might have been. There's something appalling and mysterious about an unstuffed trouser leg, in Eric's case a tube held together with three fancy safety pins, the kind usually seen at the hems of kilts. It's absence that attracts the eye. His remaining leg was hardly worthy of consideration, we kids seldom wondered how it felt, never asked ourselves did it ache in sympathy, did it pine for its partner? A shining white band would sometimes peep at us from the space between his sock and his filled trouser leg, but that was merely flesh, not nearly as absorbing as the lack on the other side of his groin. Then there was the question, not spoken aloud, but once whispered in the dark from child to child, of what happened to Eric's other shoes. This question had been hanging around, loitering with intent, for years before it made its hushed appearance. There was no sign of these surplus items, they weren't to be found, alone and dusty, under dressers or on top of wardrobes. We'd all wondered at their fate, but never dared to ask, until one day, when we were living in a little caravan at Eric and Editha's smallholding, Editha went shopping and bought Eric a new shoe. A single brown leather lace-up, size eleven. For a right foot. It was January the thirtieth, his birthday; Editha rarely shopped. I watched him unwrap his gift, give a grateful grunt, and discard his old, black, footwear to try on the new. The old shoe was put in the dustbin, although, since Eric's only journeys were from bed to chair, it wasn't exactly worn out.

That night, in our caravan, Fabian and I lay awake long after the smaller children had fallen asleep, discussing in whispers the fate of the left brown lace-up. We couldn't believe that our Granny would simply throw away a brand new leather shoe. She was, by necessity if not by nature, a thrifty soul, such waste would have seemed criminal to her.

'Maybe,' Fabe suggested, 'there's a shop for one-legged people, where they'll sell you a left shoe *or* a right one.'

'Yes,' I liked this idea, 'and they have stuff for people with only one arm too, like single gloves.'

'Maybe,' Fabe sounded unsure, 'but buying a pair of gloves isn't the same. Everybody loses gloves, but a whole shoe's different. Anyway, Gran only went to Spalding, they won't have special shops there. Only maybe in London.' Yes, in London, we'd been told, you could buy anything, from furnishings to furbelows – whatever they might be; but not in Spalding.

'Well then there's a club,' I ventured, 'and the members swap the unwanted things. This time it was Granny's turn to send somebody, a man with only a left leg, the spare shoe.

Next time it'll be his wife who has to post the right shoe to Granny.' We let this concept swim in the dark with us for a while, but it faded when we thought hard about it. Granny hadn't been seen with brown paper and string, wrapping a shoebox, and surely the box would have been used if any posting took place. In fact she'd appeared in the kitchen, having walked from the bus stop, with the single shoe in its box, and we'd been given this cardboard home to use for Stan, our pet mouse. For a few moments I saw them, an army of odd shoes, wandering tragically through shoe purgatory looking for their other halves, poor lost soles.

There was only one thing for it. We'd have to see for ourselves. The situation called for a voyage of discovery. We didn't possess slippers and there was no hope of sorting out our shoes from the pile in the caravan, so we crept across the smallholding in bare feet. The ground was white with frost. We sprang across it, as if the diamonds of ice were hot coals, until we reached the big tin dustbin. To us it felt like the dead of night, but it can't have been very late as Eric, who slept in the downstairs back room, was still awake with his light on. Good and bad luck for us. The light shone on the dustbin, making our search possible, but if Eric saw or heard us we were done for. Fabian removed the dustbin lid with the care of an expert defusing a bomb. It didn't smell too bad, Editha had a compost heap for peelings, so we leant over and began our inspection. The old black shoe was near the top only now, instead of Eric's foot, it held a sticky collection of chicken bones. Underneath was a blend of household dust, broken china, tins and something that felt horribly like a human brain. We couldn't get to the bottom, we weren't tall or brave enough to try. Fabe was about to give up when a tingling, ticklish sensation played with the back of my neck then spread right over me, and I knew suddenly that I was special, that I'd be able to see to the depths, discern the contents without actually looking, just by touching the freezing metal bin on the outside.

'Wait,' I pulled Fabian back to my side, where he sat rubbing his icy feet while I lightly fingered the dustbin. For me the pain of the cold was obliterated by the joy of discovery. I could 'see' everything, the little silver coloured toothpaste tin, two tattered, filthy hankies with 'E' for Eric embroidered in their corners, both halves of a severed dog's collar and a big lemon bath sponge.

I was lost in this magical experience; Fabe eventually had to whisper fiercely in my ear, 'What are you doing?' And then, guessing what had happened, 'Is it there?'

'No, it's not.' There was no sign of any brown shoe, I had failed to solve the mystery, but I was puffed with success, and determined to have the last word. 'But there's a three-penny piece in the pocket of that skirt Granny threw out, we could get it and spend it tomorrow.' What a generous soul. Knowing Fabe would be put out by my having magic while he had none, I did at least try to share a benefit of this wonder with him.

Back in the caravan I lay, with a sleeping sister on one side and a giant pink rabbit on the other, and felt warmed by good fortune. Tomorrow was golden with possibilities, I might do anything, see through closed doors, feel inside strangers' pockets; anything. Amazingly, brilliantly, I'd inherited some magic, and this, my Day of Discovery, was Grandad Eric's birthday so I would never forget the exact date. January the thirtieth, my own New Year's Day.

You see, it was especially exciting, because my mother had often spoken of her Day of Discovery, the day of the freak storm, and there I was, finding my own feet, yet following in her footsteps. We ought to walk home with her now, mustn't leave her standing, shaken but not scarred in the school playground.

That afternoon the children were let out early. There was no hope of calling them to order after the added excitement of visits from ambulance and fire engine. Victory travelled across a sodden landscape, veering around newly formed ponds, jumping deep puddles. She said she hadn't given her home a moment's thought, having been so pre-occupied with the dangerous roof and then having felt such empathy for Donald and his leg. But when the smallholding came into view she broke into a run and her heart pumped at double speed with a mixture of fear and relief. Relief because the place was still standing, its own tiled roof securely set where it should be. Fear because the ground was littered with debris and there was no sign of Editha.

It was then my mum knew that even if the Gypsies had brought her to Editha, and even if they reappeared one day with another 'real' mother, it was Editha she loved with a daughter's devotion. The idea that Editha might have been injured, perhaps killed during the storm was so dreadful that it stopped Victory in her tracks.

'I stood at the gate, which was alone between its two supports, the fence having been flattened, and I prayed,' she told us. I think that was the only time I heard my mother mention prayer, perhaps it was her only offering. She was a believer in many things, but not in the God of churches and prayer books.

Then she saw Editha, in the distance, a bent figure, small, busy, gathering fallen branches from the fruit trees, salvaging what she could to use for firewood.

'You all right?' Editha asked her when she came to help. 'Yes. You?'

'Bloody mess, half the crop I should say. Blown half to bits.'

And they carried on, without speaking again. They were out there clearing up until dusk, then they went in and made Eric his tea.

'He's all shook up,' Editha said in a hushed voice. Victory looked at her father who was dozing in the armchair by the stove and she wished something would shake him up, wished the storm had whipped the seat from under him, or better still, lifted him *and* his smelly old chair clean away.

My mother used to speak of Days, with a capital D. There were Days Of Deep Sorrow, which need no explanation. We had Days Of Delight, which she planned for us when we looked glum or which fell on us like presents in the post, without warning. We enjoyed Good Food Days and Glad Days and Sad Days. And she spoke of the day of the freak storm as a Day Of Discovery because not only did her feelings for Editha define themselves and settle down, but she also found out how far reaching her magic really was. Until then it had been a toy almost, a bag of tricks with which to plague the enemy. Now she knew what strength she possessed, what pain it might bring, and how little she could do, even when a warning came so clearly, to stop the inevitable.

Those of us who know in advance that death threatens or disaster is on the way are bound to suffer from the burden of guilt. I used to worry myself to a state of sickness as a child because I could see it, a fire, a flood or whatever, coming, and do nothing about it. But my mother taught me not to blame myself when stories I had 'invented' appeared later as articles in newspapers. I accepted my talent easily enough though, children do. I never found the magic itself surprising; which makes it hard to understand why the rest of the human race can't come to terms with the fact that some of us are born with a gift for music, say, or mathematics, and some of us are able to see a little further, do a little more than average. The only time I'm surprised is when my magic lets me down, as it did today.

There are so many questions I'd like to ask you, Matthew. But even on paper I am shy of being forward. I suppose the only enquiry that matters is whether or not you want me to carry on telling you about myself and my family? Of course I hope you'll say yes, and accept the gift of somebody who wants to be, to begin with, your friend at least. Your eyes, which I believe I only dared to meet the once, struck me as intelligent and deeply understanding. You'll have got the gist.

I wait for your answer, eagerly, apprehensively and, being a born optimist, hopefully.

I wait; what else can a prisoner do?

Three

I have your letter here. Of course it delights me, this paper and these words. You tell me all the right things; you want to hear more of my family, learn more about me.

But to see you again, well, I had hoped. Stupid of me I know, but I'd imagined another meeting, less formal – although I understand that cosiness is hard to achieve in a prison Visitors' Room, surrounded by other couples. Still, I'd pictured us, myself groomed this time but shyly blushing, having a conversation practically as normal people do. Watching each other's mannerisms, you perhaps smoothing your almost shaved, thinning hair while I ran my fingers through my tangled mane. Smiling at the many contradictions. Basically, getting to know each other in that ordinary but exciting way. We shall have to have another chat, you can't give up on me now, we must meet eyeball to eyeball again sometime. Your letter decimates any chance that meeting might have had of being informal or without embarrassment. Before I got your reply I was looking forward to the next time; now I rather dread seeing you again.

I have alarmed you. I never intended to do that.

Also your letter leaves me in the same one-sided tell-all

situation. Oh, now I'm assured that you're happy to read my words, and that's a relief all right. But I still know next to nothing about you. I search the letter for clues. Good quality paper, the colour of a spring sky. I bet ... yes, there it is, Basildon Bond watermarked right through. A man of taste and big-hearted enough to find me worthy of expensive paper. There is a very faint smell, not of perfume or after-shave. I think it's that pot-pourri stuff people have taken to having in their rooms. A Christmas present? Or did you buy it, bending to sniff the varieties carefully before selecting this subtle lime and spice mixture?

You, who walk about freely, can have no idea how I long to do something as mundane as shopping. I never was a great one for buying anything before, but now, oh to be able to choose, to make decisions about colours and textures. Best of all would be the chance to shop with you. To stand by as you picked oranges from a basket. I haven't told you how impressed I was with your hands, have I? Long fingers. Do you play the piano, Matthew? You should, otherwise you're wasting a great set of digits. When I close my eyes I can still see your clean pink fingers, topped by white, white crescent moons that seem to glow in the dark.

Your handwriting ought to tell me plenty, but I'm no expert. I suppose the long upward lines of your 't's and 'l's means you are reaching for the sky, a dreamer. Your 'o's are perfect, pure, like the mouths of choir boys singing. My writing puts me to shame. It's so big. I must seem over-confident to any reader, but in fact I write this way for the simplest of reasons. In school our homework was always supposed to cover two sides of a page. If I covered the paper quickly I had more time to play. My mum used to tell me not to bother sending postcards when I went away. 'They only make them big enough for you to write the address,' she'd say, 'and we already know where we live.'

You write with a fountain pen, a proper pen of the kind never to be found amongst the chewed pencils and snapped crayons in our house. No nib could have survived my brother Merry's inspection anyway. I was once ordered to use a pen at school, but leaking ink stained my fingers and puddled my pages, so I was allowed to use a biro. But I can see the attraction now, I love the way the ink becomes integrated with the paper rather than merely resting on it.

I can't believe I'm waxing lyrical about a pen. God help me.

Your letter wasn't posted, it was delivered by hand. Which means you must have been here yesterday. I hadn't thought about you having other, what are we? Clients? Cases? Not here, anyway, under the same roof as me. Useless to pretend I don't care, that I'm not jealous: my envy will seep into this writing like a bad smell. Who is she, or who are they? These others who have your attention? Not that names would mean anything to me. I am still the new girl, I've hardly spoken to a soul, including you, since I got here. Until today that suited me fine. The last thing I wanted was to get into conversation, to have to start explaining myself, talking about my mother to strangers and listening to their own stories or excuses. Now I wish I knew the finer details of each case, not only why they are here but who comes to comfort them. I want to study the face of whoever it was you came to visit yesterday, to see what I'm up against.

Actually, I lie. I have spoken to one woman. She's a bull, the kind I used to protect my son against when he was tiny.

On Saturdays we get extra rations, little packets of biscuits to keep, to take to our cells and hoard for special moments. With a stomach like mine, there's no shortage of such moments and my Rich Teas were a treasure beyond price. This woman wanted them, hinting that it'd be in my best interests to hand them over without a fuss.

'They're a tax,' she said, 'sort of like insurance.'

I told her I didn't believe in paying taxes and suggested a part of her anatomy into which she might stuff her collection of biscuits. For my trouble I got a quick clip round the ear, deftly delivered out of sight of any warders. The sting made me proud of my tenacity; as I ate them that night under cover of darkness, the biscuits tasted sweeter for the fight.

I wish I'd seen you. I'd have been delighted by the merest glimpse of your small, neat body as it turned a corner. But more than that, I wish I'd known. Your having been in the building, seeing another and delivering a letter to me, without my knowing about it, this is further depressing proof that, where you're concerned, my magic has stopped working. And that is scary. For somebody who's always had the power to see trouble or happiness coming, and a mother who could do something about it, to find herself motherless and powerless is the loneliest of feelings.

It seems I'm on my own, no hope of beguiling you with the trickery that's worked so well for me in the past. I once told my mum about a boy, Ben Davidson – the focus of many a fifth-former's dreams. I told her he walked right by me at school, didn't even know I existed, a situation which was breaking my tender, inexperienced heart. We devised this plan, Mum and I. When he was nearby I was to tell her, telepathically of course since she was at home and I was suffering the indignities of the local comprehensive. Her magic was always more effective than mine. While I could only feel his approach, she had the ability, even at a distance, to control his shoes. For a few glorious days, until I realized his soul in no way matched the beauty of his eyes, that behind his knee-watering looks there lurked the dull, grey brain of a future insurance broker, I enjoyed long minutes of Ben Davidson's undivided attention. He was unwittingly brought to me, his footsteps carrying him to within an inch of my face where they would halt, his black suede shoes stuck fast to the spot. I saw a great deal of the inside of Ben's mouth – a vision which finally helped me to fall out of lust with him – in those spell-bound minutes. He invariably left this orifice hanging open while I engaged in light, and I hoped entertaining conversation of the 'chatting up' variety. I soon told my mother to stop bothering with him, that he had no personality and nothing to say for himself.

'Just shows,' she teased, 'you can take a man to the daughter, but you can't make him think.'

Still, long after I had lost interest in Ben, I would see him coming and mutter, 'Oh no, here comes the most moronic mouth in school,' and his shoes would swivel in my direction or turn him round and round confusingly.

Perhaps, in this instance and this instance only, I'm better off without my mother's help. I want you to come to me of your own free will. Frightening as it is, I do rather relish the challenge of getting your interest by fair means. Nothing but my own, tubby, untidy self with which to lure you. Not doing too well so far, am I? One short but beautifully written letter to my credit, and reading the sky-blue spaces, between the lines, it seems, understandably, that I only became interesting after my mother's death. But I'm writing this to show that I am more than just a case. I am Eve, with a long history and a personality which goes way beyond my crime. And you must see me Matthew. Consider me at least before accepting or rejecting me, before moving on to other women.

In spite of all my lumps and bumps, I've never been seriously unhappy with the way I look. I'd be uneasy in a different body, uncomfortable with a more perfect face. But right now I wish I was saturated with sex appeal. Somewhere along the line, I've missed out there, because my mother, when young, must have had enough of this magnetism to pull an army. Not everybody realized this, because she never flaunted her appeal once she'd finished having her tribe of kids. I know some people, the teachers who dealt with seven children from the one mother and a heptad of fathers for example, thought my mum must have been so unappealing that she couldn't keep a man for weeks let alone years. But there's always two ways of seeing things; to my mind, my mother was so sexy that seven men, at least seven, found her irresistible and made love to her with the kind of passion I have always believed it takes, although I know this belief is unfounded, to make babies. Seven men in quick succession, one passion hotly following the next. What a variety of men too. We kids had a wondrous, colourful selection of dads. True, many of the attributes we bestowed on these men were sheer inventions – for example Fabian, the eldest of my four brothers, insisted he was fathered by a particularly enigmatic rock guitarist – but their physical glories, passed on to us, are there for all the world to see.

I suppose it's hardly surprising that having seven babies changed my mother. She had us in quick succession. I was just eight when Samik, the youngest, arrived, and so I only know the Victory who vamped about before she became a multi-mother from stories, fragments of memories told by Mum herself or laughed over with her friend Taff – whenever the two of them got together.

When asked why she had so many kids, my mother would say it was all on account of her magnetism. But did she mean simply sexual attraction? Or was she talking about a biological pull? Perhaps, when she reached a certain age, she found that she conceived every time she had sex. Or almost. Was it her ovaries that held the magic magnetism, boasting the suction of a vacuum cleaner so that any sperm, having been shot from his safe haven, found escape impossible? Then again she might have meant something else entirely; she may have been suggesting that children found her mixture of mothering and magic so delightful that they were queuing up to be conceived by her. I have pictured this scene, a row of little souls, arms waving eagerly in the misty air of children's heaven, all trying to catch the attention of the dark, twinkling lady. Any of these explanations might be right in terms of what my mother meant. That's the way it was with Victory, everything she said had many connotations each of which, at a given time, could be the logical answer.

Although I don't suppose Taff was around every time my mother conceived, carried, or produced one of us, I find it hard to separate her from scenes of love, sex and courtship. Victory and Taff met in their fourteenth year and stayed close as underwear to skin right through 'til Victory's death. Taff is still going strong, a fat, toothless old bag with an outrageous laugh and a way of finding the innuendo in any phrase or sentence. I haven't seen her since my mother died. The prospect sickens me but I suppose we'll have to meet again soon; Taff wouldn't miss the court case if she was in an iron lung – but in fact her lungs are working all too well in spite of her chain-smoking and having lived, until being recently moved to a Home, on a busy main road. They'll have to gag her, no amount of shouting 'order please' will have any effect on Taff. Who needs a prosecution counsel when they can rely on the best friend of the deceased to yell abuse? Apart from her anger and hatred, I'm afraid of confronting Taff's grief. She can't possibly be as lost and empty as I am but she'll make such a show it'll put the rest of us to shame.

There never was much love lost between us. We were rivals, I suppose, vying for the position of top place in Victory's affections. When Taff came to visit, we children felt pushed aside. She'd take up two easy chairs, her great bum bulging in one while her bad legs rested on another, and smoke us all out of the room. From our place of banishment we'd hear her cackling and we'd plot all kinds of torments for her. But Taff had Victory's protection. Our minor tortures were sometimes successful; we made superb slings from her giant knickers and once persuaded her to eat cubes of Ex-Lax, which she mistook for plain chocolate. But our plans for major horrors were always thwarted because, without necessarily seeing for herself, Victory knew what was what:

'No Taff, not that chair, I think you'll find it's booby-trapped with drawing pins.'

They never bore us any malice, Taff and Victory. To them, kids would be little terrors. They'd have found us far more offensive if we'd tip-toed about being good and nice. I know this is true because my mother fretted more over Perdita in her perfect stage than she ever did over the troubles the rest of us brought on her and on ourselves. I shouldn't hold Taff's friendship with my mother against her. Not having been a mother herself, Taff did her best to be an aunty, treating us to mountains of takeaway food and trailing big but hopeless presents in her wake. Large stuffed animals were favourites, mostly orange and yellow monsters she'd won at Bingo, another of Taff's addictions. One such creature, sporting a vast red baseball cap, was blocking out the draft by the back door of The Cornflake House to the bitter end.

When they first met, Victory and Taff had a lot more than their shared age in common. Both girls had suffered friendless childhoods, a bond which instantly cemented their relationship. Like Victory, Taff was an outsider. Worse, sin of sins, she was actually a foreigner. Her full name was Myfanwy and she was half Welsh. Although she had only the faintest of accents, her voice was ridiculed by other children. Taff reckons this never bothered her, sticks and stones and so on; and it's hard to imagine her sulking or giving a damn, but it did set her apart. Taff is as down to earth as Victory was up in the clouds. She says exactly what she thinks, gets into endless trouble and laughs fit to bust at those who don't like it. The two adolescents seemed made for each other, two halves of an invincible whole. Heaven help those who stood in their way as they bucked and pranced from child to adulthood.

'We met at dancing classes,' one or the other of them would tell us again and again, 'no boy was ever brave enough to take either of us in his arms, we looked a sorry sight in those days. So there we were, four sets of toes in tight shoes, two breasts colliding to the strains of the foxtrot. Most of the class we spent doubled up with giggles or the stitch. Seemed to dance everything at breakneck speed, didn't we Dear? Not a glimmer of timing between us. Often enough we'd finished, worn ourselves out, halfway through the music. Still, the best bit was sitting, panting and watching to see whose hands were sliding towards whose bum, whose trousers boasted the biggest bulge.'

I can hear Taff's laugh now, as clearly as if she was in the next cell. A laugh to shake solid walls.

To be fair, Taff did practise refinement from time to time, and it took some practise I'm sure. She had no choice, few men would have looked at her in her natural state. And she loved men. Or I should say she loves them; I'm sure she's flirting still in her old folks' home, exercising those heavy eyelids whenever a bloke walks by. Toning down the cackle until it sounds more ladylike. Give her a couple of vodka tonics and you'll hear the real thing but by then with any luck you'll be pissed too and that'll soften the edges.

Can you see them? Those two almost-women, dancing together out of time, whizzing round the floor of some dusty old hall in the hope of hurrying the arrival of love and sex? It couldn't come quickly enough for them, they were, in all senses, ahead of their time.

I know my problem. I want to be Taff, in those good old days. I want to giggle with Victory at the boys in all their gawky glory, to feel my knees knock in harmony with hers when a handsome one appears on the scene. To triumph over the good girls, over the prigs in permanent waves. To swing down the street after the rain, a shining girl on the arms of a likely lad, orange lights reflected in the puddles, my stockings damp, my body ready. I want to be there, taking life in great gulps, not being for one second a tease, but offering and accepting the real thing. Going all the way.

There you go Matthew, another window opens and you see yet another of my secrets, more of my soul.

My cell mate Liz has had some post too. Hers must contain the kind of news she'd rather not have known. Her eyes are red, her mouth is down at the corners. From time to time, I look up and give her what I hope is a sympathetic smile but she ignores me.

Ah well, back to that other pair. Yes, Taff and Victory were alike, but they were opposites too, as friends perhaps ought to be.

Well, I say that Victory was a friendless child, but after the freak storm she grew very close to her mother, Editha, or rather very fond of her. Being loved and appreciated was such a novelty for Editha – the experience came too late for her to enjoy it wholeheartedly. She never achieved that easy, confidential, giggling state that I enjoyed with my mum. There was always a brusqueness about Granny which gave the impression that she didn't care. But we knew she loved Victory and us grandchildren really, deep down, because nothing, not her silent hard-working father, not the endless storms and gales she suffered or the routine of her life, not even her lazy demanding husband, could take the softness out of Editha's smile. I think my grandmother found the seven of us heavy going, but also awe inspiring. She was nosy, interfering and bloody-minded in her old age but she had a way of staring at one or the other of us as if we'd dropped from outer space and then breaking into that special smile of hers which was composed of nothing more or less complicated than inherent love.

While she was still at junior school, my mother did form one friendship, another rapport that sprung from the Day of Discovery, the freak storm day. Miss Downy was won over by Victory when the weather calmed. The child she'd seen as a trial was clearly blessed with the gift of vision; and who in their right minds would carry on treating one so talented as the enemy? Miss Downy waved the white flag and crossed No Man's Land with all the caution of one who knows the territory is explosive.

'Although I thought she dealt with Kathleen, Donald and the roof-tunnel fearlessly,' my mother told me, 'Miss Downy wasn't a naturally brave woman. She was not so much blonde as white, I never saw hair as pale or skin so clear. When embarrassed she would blush to the roots of that lemon hair and when she was frightened she blanched to the point of transparency. After the storm she was alternately embarrassed and afraid of me, flashing hot and cold alarmingly throughout lessons. Before long the whole class would be watching for the colour changes, nudging each other when the first signs appeared and wearing out red crayons doing cartoons of her face. She was on the verge of losing control when I took pity on her and gave her the stone. It was nothing really, just a peachy pebble, but I said it was a crystal and would bring her luck. The important thing was that she understood it to be a peace offering, which it was. It did bring her respite from the flushes and freezes, which was the kind of peace she wanted and it did bring her luck, of a sort. A couple of days later she met a man who found her see-through skin and limpid hair attractive. Within weeks she was blushing more than ever, but from joyful embarrassment this time, and hinting that we might be calling her something other than Miss Downy by the start of the following term.'

It didn't last. I forget why, the man fell out of love perhaps, with Miss Downy or with the bleakness of the area. Anyway he moved on. My mother arrived at school one autumn day with a bunch of chrysanthemums for her teacher.

'It's sweet of you, Victory,' Miss Downy thanked her, 'but there's no need. It's not a special occasion.'

'You might be glad of them tomorrow,' Victory muttered, 'they'll help to cheer you up.'

The next morning Miss Downy had sore, red eyes with which she kept peeping at the 'Dear John' letter in her cardigan pocket. This time she didn't hold Victory's clairvoyancy against her, she just smiled sadly whenever she caught the little girl's eye.

'We were on good terms right until I left that school,' my mother assured us, 'and when I went she gave me the McDuff Egg.'

At this point in the story Mum would usually hunt for the tiny tartan egg, and if it could be found amongst the clutter she'd hold it up as if offering it for auction. The McDuff Egg was a masterpiece in miniaturization and ingenuity. Made of wood, it hatched, when twisted, to reveal a complete sewing kit with a thimble in the bulbous end of the egg and threads spooled around a central stem that housed pins and needles. Some of the weave in the tartan was outlined in gold, and the name McDuff was written amongst the reds and greens in minuscule golden lettering. My mother had a wicker basket full of impossible tangles of cottons, fat, lethal pin cushions, needle cases shaped like fruits or many skirted ladies, and this she used, diving in to its dangerous depths whenever we ripped or burst out of our clothes. But the McDuff Egg was complete and untouched even when ... Oh God, I suppose I should have saved it. I never thought ... Zulema was especially fond of it, she has small, neat hands – although she used to spoil these by constantly chewing her nails – she's always liked objects that fit snugly in her palm.

A terrible thing is happening to me, Matthew. The lining of my stomach is starting to eat itself up. I am sick and my insides are hollow. I suppose you will guess this feeling is guilt, or its little brother, remorse. But it is neither; it is dread, catching up with me at last. You must encounter this all the time, people who are ill with fear. Even though I'm sitting down, dizziness is throwing me off balance. What have I done? What am I doing here? Why haven't I asked myself these questions before? I didn't care, my mother was dying, then she was dead and I didn't care where I went from there. Coming here, it didn't matter. I hardly gave it a thought; prison. Or if I was capable of giving thoughts to any kind of future, I assumed that prison would be a good place for me. I wanted the distance, the locked doors. It was away from them, that was the essential thing.

I can't believe my mother is dead. Although I've missed her, cried over her, suffered from her absence; I haven't believed in it, death, the fact that I will never see her again. My subconscious expects her to appear, in this cell, or later, at my trial. When I saw your letter I thought for one second . . . I jump when I hear the distant ring of the telephone, still hoping . . . My ears are strained for the first sound of her voice, a voice that will speak up for me when everybody else talks of me with hatred and anger. But she isn't here, and she will not be there, will she Matthew? She's gone.

For the first time I am taking in my surroundings. Why did they send me to this place and not to an open prison? Am I so evil, in their eyes, that I can't be trusted? Why doesn't Liz want to speak to me? I'm not used to silence. I was brought up in The Cornflake House, for God's sake, where every room rang with cries, laughter, music. And bare walls, just this yellowing paint all over the place, not a picture to look at, when I'm used to postcards by the yard, beer mats stuck to every surface and a ceiling decorated with cut out planets and stars.

I have nothing but your letter. Not one piece of junk to gaze at or to hold. Not a single memento. My own fault, of course, if we are talking of blame. Once the shock has worn off, my family may come to visit me and I cannot face them alone. How can I be expected to see them, to answer their accusations, with nothing in my pockets? My mother understood this need and passed her understanding and her tokens on to those she cared for. Please visit me first, Matthew, before my brothers and sisters come, and please bring me something solid. A pebble or a painted egg, something which fits comfortably in my hand. No matter what they say is right, or what they think is wrong, there is a limit to the punishment a person can take. I am sorry, if being sorry will help my cause; but in the name of justice, there is a limit.

Bring me an object, Matthew, a token of friendship. I'm a companionable soul, I wasn't designed to be this empty and alone.

Four

Too late, Matthew. Even if you are walking my way as you read this, it is too late. I have had my visitor. Need I say how my heart lifted when I was told that somebody wanted to see me? I assumed it would be you, preened myself in readiness, swallowed the lump in my throat so that this time I might be able to speak to you. I was so intent on looking for your compact, delightful form, that at first I didn't notice my own son waiting for me. Mind you, my son was the last person I expected to see – and besides, he had changed beyond all recognition. His hair, which should be as golden as mine, now looks like the aftermath of a failed chemistry experiment.

Did I already mention my great big, baby boy? If not let me say now that I'm blessed with one son, aged eighteen, who likes to be known as Bing. Maybe I should add that I've been a rather average mother and consequently my son has managed, in his comparatively short life, to get himself into a great deal of trouble. Whatever; he's a sweet boy. Not about to win any prizes for conversation or deportment, but basically sound.

We were shy as strangers with each other. Then he said what I was thinking:

'This is weird, Mum. Wrong way round, you inside, me visiting.'

It was a long speech for him.

I was suddenly overjoyed to see him and deeply moved by the effort he'd made to get all this way from wherever he'd been hiding. I muttered words to this effect and he mumbled that, as luck would have it, he hadn't been that far from his dear old mum. He was living about twenty miles away, down a hole, under a stretch of land that will inevitably become part of a bypass. So that was why he smelt, amongst other things, of damp clay. His fingernails, when I focused on them, were the colour of weather-beaten flower pots. I wondered how deep his hole might be and does he feel safe there, being separated from the world? Safe as I felt when I first came here? Or does he expect the world to fall on his head any minute? Then I thought this; the point of protest by burrowing was surely to stay underground until the last minute, so as to make headlines, drawing attention to your cause by being dragged out triumphantly in front of flash-lights and reporters. By surfacing prematurely, he had made a heart-rending sacrifice on my behalf.

'You came up . . . just for me,' I said, almost overwhelmed by motherly love. 'Oh, Ble . . .' but he stopped me there. And we were back at loggerheads, where we are actually more comfortable with each other than on the cosy but foreign ground of caring and showing it. I'd been about to call him by his full, his proper name. He hates that.

'It seems I'm in deep shit,' I smiled at myself for using his vocabulary.

'Yeah.'

'Have you seen any of them?' Meaning his aunts, uncles and cousins.

'Nah.'

'No, well, I guess not, living in a hole.'

My son grinned and I noticed that he has chipped yet another of his teeth.

'Do you eat enough?'

He laid his hands on his stomach, resting his case: not a strong argument since his figure resembles an army-booted bean-pole. I didn't need to ask if he was able to wash himself underground. The answer had been wafting my way each time I inhaled. Still, he looked great to me, blinded as I was by emotion, and I could have held my breath and hugged him, had we been on hugging terms. It occurred to me that I looked like the 'before' in one of those magazine articles anyway; we deserved each other. I still couldn't get over the fact that he'd come, clay, hair, smells and all, to visit me. Appreciation and wonder made me dumb. He played the edge of the table that divided us, fingers hitting an imaginary keyboard as our eyes tried to avoid the sting of meeting. In that silence I felt as if every emotion had chosen my heart in which to settle. And amongst this rabble of emotions, was a newcomer; pride. I was proud of him, of his protest and his essential goodness, even of the way he looked. He hides a well-shaped face behind the stubble, fine bones and a neat nose. His eyes are dark green and, in spite of all his efforts to be laid back, full of intensity. Of course I've always loved him, it's just that I wasn't always there for him, to borrow a phrase from the Yanks. Yet he was being there for me; and his physical presence meant more than any letter, Matthew, no matter how pretty or expensive the paper.

As I looked at Bing, I remembered how I used to fret over him when he was a child. I always knew when he was in trouble or in danger but I wasn't always able to do anything about it. And I thought of other mothers, because I'd heard, in schools and playgroups, mention of premonitions concerning children. It seems women often know when their offspring are threatened. They *know*, without the phone call or the knock on the door, that something is wrong. I've heard of many cases personally. Women who stayed home, putting off the weekly shop because they'd be needed sooner rather than later. Mothers who took themselves to Casualty without being told, knowing their child was also on the way, in the back of an ambulance. I saw a woman double up with pain one morning and discovered next day that her daughter had developed appendicitis. We accept warnings like these, we may mull over them, perhaps even marvel at them, but we don't raise our arms in disbelief or horror. Now can you see why I found it easy to accept my magic? If you believe in one drop of water, and if you have no problem coming to terms with streams and brooks, then rivers shouldn't give you that much trouble.

'I can't believe you came . . .' I said to Bing because it was true and I could think of nothing else to say. I remembered having used the same phrase to Oliver, my son's father, nearly nineteen years ago. Oliver had appeared on the doorstep of The Cornflake House on the very day I was preparing to go to a clinic and have an abortion. My son was literally saved by the bell, the ghastly 'Avon calling' chimes which heralded the arrival of the man responsible for my pregnant state. Oliver had a hare-lip, or he had been born with one. An operation to free the lip had left him with a twist to his mouth and a lisp to his speech which I found impossibly arousing. I was so in love, I remember confusion and sickness, the joy of touching, the pain of parting. We did more parting than touching, a sure sign that our love affair was doomed. But on that day Oliver came to see me.

'I can't believe you came...' I gasped. Then we talked; and he convinced me to keep the baby by promising that I would have his manly support – not only throughout my pregnancy but for ever and always.

To be fair to the man, he did reappear occasionally to pat my pod of a stomach and offer words of encouragement. I knew he was dating a thinner, less encumbered blonde by the time I gave birth, but he made an effort and turned up to see me while I was in the maternity ward.

'Well done, Sweetie,' he lisped, as if I'd won a horse race. I grinned. I've always had a thing about men's voices; some, like yours Matthew, are smooth plain chocolate to the hungry senses. Oliver could have talked me into anything – well, I suppose that was how I came to be there, between maternity ward sheets, in the first place. He told me he thought I should call the tiny new being Trevor, an idea that made me laugh out loud until I realized he'd said, 'I think *you* should call him Trevor,' rather than 'I think *we* should.' He clearly had no intention of being part of any decision making team. I said I'd already decided on a name and when I told him my choice, it was Oliver's turn to laugh loudly. A reaction that's been echoed by many equally small-minded people since.

'It's quite common in Africa,' I sulked, but this only made Oliver scoff some more.

The last time I saw Oliver was by accident. In fact it

almost caused an accident. I was being given a lift by a friend and when we stopped at a junction, I looked to my side and there he was, in a parallel car, tanned, handsome, carefree as ever. I gasped and my companion's foot slipped off the clutch, making us shoot forward until we almost hit a lorry. Oliver didn't see me, he was busy talking into a mobile phone.

I've often wondered why Oliver bothered to stop me from having an abortion. Did he want a child simply so that he could boast of having fathered 'some kid somewhere'? Or was he spurred by the basic instinct to procreate the species? Maybe he was just proud of being fertile. Or possibly, and this only occurred to me recently, my mother took control of his shoes too, so that, like Ben Davidson, he was forced to confront me.

I was still gazing fondly at the silent piano player's fingernails.

'You were a love child,' I said softly, 'did I ever tell you that before?'

'Yeah,' but he looked glad to hear it again.

A fresh thought occurred to me, 'How did you hear about me? About all of it?'

He hadn't seen any of his relations and he could hardly have been watching television in his cave.

'Papers,' he explained, 'big spread and a picture in the locals, little para in a national.' Yes, of course he'd be getting the newspapers, or having them delivered. I found myself whimsically wondering if his hole had an address. It must have been a shock, searching for articles about himself and his fellow protesters but finding a 'big spread' about his errant mother. As if he'd read my thoughts, he said, 'We were in together, one day, you and me.'

'Ah,' I thought this was rather touching, two lawbreakers united by the snipe and snap of the press.

The look on my face must have prompted him, in this strange about-turn situation, to ask what any responsible prison visitor should.

'Why? Why did you do it?'

I was tempted to answer, flippantly, that it had seemed a good idea at the time, because this had been *his* response when I'd once asked him the same question. He's always been anti motor cars and when he was asked 'Why did you do it?', he'd just punctured every tyre in our neighbourhood. Not only that, but he'd been caught doing so. Still, this was a whole lot more serious and he deserved a decent answer, 'I did it for her, for your Grandma Victory.' I found it impossible to say more, my throat itched, my eyes prickled and I so badly wanted to avoid tears.

'Fair enough,' he said. I loved him the most then, more than I knew I could.

Our time was up. We were standing, smiling gently at each other.

'Do you hug?' I asked.

He responded as if I'd invited him to dance.

'You asking?'

'I'm asking.'

'Well, I'm hugging.'

I expect, I hope, that I still smell of him, of his earthy hideout and his unwashed hair, of his roll-ups and his age-old combat trousers. No perfume could have been sweeter to me. Back in my cell, holding him again and again in my memory, I find it impossible to think of him as Bing. It just doesn't suit him. He chose it because it consists of four of the letters of his whole name. Other possibilities were Les, Sin or Sing and, one which had us rolling with mirth, Bess. I can't say I blame him for discarding the name I chose for him. I suppose I was hoping to follow in my mother's footsteps, give my child a head start in being extraordinary, but now I can see that I went too far. Mind you, my boy didn't shrink from me as I whispered his name in his ear while enjoying that long, lovely hug:

'Thank you, Blessing,' I dared to offer. 'Thank you for this show of strength.'

Eighteen years ago, when Oliver had disappeared through the swing doors of the maternity ward and the echo of his scorn had died away, I lay with Blessing in my arms and wept. Of course I felt abandoned, heavy with the tragedy of unrequited love; but now I understand that those were probably just the usual post-natal tears, brought about by dancing hormones. I don't cry easily or frequently. Only birth and death seem to affect my tear ducts. And before long I felt a gratifying grain of grit mixed with the salt on my cheeks. I knew I'd get by without a man – but I was no fool, I understood that it wouldn't be easy. I'd watched my mother struggle the same way. I looked down at baby Blessing's fuzzy head. 'Son,' I told him, 'you'd better live up to that name of yours.'

Today, at last, my Blessing has proved that he was listening to me all that time ago.

Five

Thank you, Matthew, for your visit and for my frog. I can honestly say I like nothing better than this tiny creature. I love his polished colours, shades of damp forest floors, moss, ivy and periwinkle. Being made of stone, being the colour of plants and shaped in the image of a living thing, he brings all aspects of the outside world into my cell. What a clever man you are. You knew, before I knew myself, that a smooth, stone frog was exactly what I most wanted. He sits in my palm, happy as any of his living brothers and sisters on their lily pads.

See, I was right about you all along. You've proved that you have a heart. Please don't panic when you read this. I understand that the frog is only a token of your sympathy. I heard what you said; it's impossible for you to see me at any time other than on your official visits. And you must stick to only a professional relationship with an inmate. Understood. Honestly. You can relax in the certain knowledge that I'm not about to leap up and ravish you – much as the idea appeals. I'll practise restraint. But things change; all things change all the time. I won't always be here, on the wrong side of the law, gazing longingly at you, on the right side. When they hear my full story, they'll throw my case out of court. If I hadn't been incoherent with grief, I should have explained myself on the night of my arrest, and most likely I'd have been freed on the spot. You see, although my action was dramatic, in a place where drama is abhorred, I hardly think of it as a crime at all.

I had a visit from my solicitor, my brief as they say. She's not quite the forceful character a person in prison would chose. Dress wise, she reminded me of Perdita, my smart, businesslike younger sister, the same neat blouse and tight black skirt. My sister. Sometimes I think Perdita must have been a foundling, she's so unlike the rest of us. Apart from the clothes, my solicitor is softer than my sister, I can't imagine her standing up for me in court. Not that she doesn't have my interest at heart, but she waffles. I did my best to reassure her, explaining that all I need is the chance to tell my tale but she gave me the impression she wasn't quite listening. Her name is Valerie and she has dark, frizzy hair and very white skin which is flecked with moles. Because her voice is so monotonous, my mind kept wandering.

I thought it was a shame Mum hadn't met her. My mother had a way with moles. She had to find some excuse to touch them, which caused problems when they were in awkward places, but once she'd laid her hands on those brown growths, they faded away. Spots and warts also succumbed to her touch. We children had the clearest skins in the county.

I once saw my mum grab a teenage boy in the street. A risky business because he was with a gang of his leather-clad mates at the time. She held his face in her hands. 'Sorry,' she told him, moving her fingers over to the screaming patch of acne near his nose, 'I thought you were one of my brood,' and she patted him as old people pat toddlers, 'but I expect you've got a perfectly good mother of your own at home.'

His companions hardly had time to be derisive as she walked away. Within seconds they were gawping at the magical vanishing of their friend's pimples, craters and humps.

Valerie droned on, being despondent, but I couldn't concentrate. I gave her my most reassuring smile as I thought about moles and frogs. I'm so proud of myself because, in spite of everything, I saw, and fell for, the frog-giver in you.

Scottie dogs and frogs. What else do you like, Matthew? Possibly, hopefully, snogs? Oh God, if I could only sit by you in a pub, drinking beer, giggling, teasing, watching you as you got to know me. I'd be so damn proud to be out with you. I should glow like a lump of plutonium. Still, we did it, eh? We met. We talked; and I didn't die of embarrassment. Not quite. You can have no idea how tantalizing it was, seeing you again, or how nerve-racking. It was almost impossible to make the journey from cell to Visitors' Room, my legs became rubber tubes, my heart a dinner gong. Didn't you hear its reverberations? How polite and wonderfully understated you are. That's a large part of your appeal for me.

How to explain this attraction? It's you, Matthew, the whole you, I've fallen for. That cleanliness, that care, attention to detail, I find it simply melts me. Maybe you'll never fully understand, you'd need not only to stand back from your own self, to look with my eyes at the neat, appealing man opposite me, but also to go backwards, to step inside my old life in an impossible way. Imagine being one of seven children, one of whom was seriously deranged, for a start. Think of the noise, the constant cries, discordant music, slamming doors, calls for help, barking dogs, telephone bells. I used to sing to myself as a child, any old song, the jollier the better, to drown the others out.

'We're off to see the wizard . . .'

'Muuummm!'

'Wahhhh!'

'. . . the wonderful wizard of Oz . . .'

'Brrring, brrring!'

'Woof, woof, woof!'

'. . . if ever a wiz of a wiz there was . . .'

I was pink with indignation when it was me, tuneful, cheerful me, they told to shut up. Then along comes this quiet, gentle man with a name that sounds like pure relief; Maff-phew. So soft after the cacophony of such a childhood.

Now try inhaling the smells. Tea-towels boiling, fish frying, nappies stinking. Bend close to the floor if you dare, get a whiff of that carpet, soaked in years of animal and human excrement. Sorry, but my brother Merry never did get the hang of toilets. Upstairs there's a heady mixture of perfumes, teenage boys' aftershaves, nail polish, cheap violet scent, talcum powder and that unmistakable smell you get from gerbils kept in small bedrooms. No wonder I'm thrilled by the fragrance of a manly bar of cream soap, which is all I detect about your person.

Then there was the untidiness. My mother tried, she wasn't slovenly, you wouldn't have called her house-proud but she did make some effort to keep those corners clean. It was a losing battle though. The Cornflake House was an average size, not a great rambling home for a hatch of children. We fell over each other and each other's toys constantly. Tables and chairs were hidden under books, papers, security blankets. Until I started dating and visiting, I'd never sat down without first shifting a pile of junk. To emerge from a home like that in pressed, unsoiled clothing, in shoes with matching laces, was unfeasible. We were the misfits, the new scruffs on the block. Rainbow coloured, unelasticated, tied together with bits of chewed string. We were reliably, consistently messy. You could depend on The Cornflake House kids to turn up for PE with one brown and one grey plimsoll, to appear in assembly wearing the wrong school tie. I will never be groomed, I wasn't made that way, but I could happily bask in your spruceness, Matthew. Forgive me for getting personal, but I appreciate your form to the point where I know that you have what is, to me, a perfect body. You would be tidy even in the nude.

At least this time I made an effort and was prepared, as best I could be. I wonder if you noticed the brushed hair and teeth, the pearls? Thank God I sat behind myself, not able to see what you saw. Imagine if we'd been designed differently, how terrible to have to watch every blush and frown, every slackening of our own jaws. Talking of blushes, do you know that your cheeks redden exquisitely under stress? A trait we have in common, at last. I'd thought we might be too precisely opposite. When you shook my hand, secreting my frog there, your jaw, which is very fine by the way, sharply outlined, twitched just a little and your complexion darkened in a way that made me long for a fan to cool you. I can't bear it now, the distance of the law between us. Keeping my distance, trying to win you without being able to make contact, this is the second most difficult thing I have ever had to do. Perhaps life will always be this hard on me now; the second most difficult quest is following so closely on the heels of the first. I only hope that captivating you doesn't bring me as fierce a punishment as the one I am suffering for freeing my mother.

You said you wanted me to try and tell you about myself as a child, to explain how it felt to be Eve, the eldest. It felt brilliant and tragic, marvellous and ordinary. I was both princess and pauper, a clumsy tub with a thin, dainty girl locked inside. A kid who never cared about clothes, yet longed for lace, silk, sequins. Well what child isn't a mass, or in my case a mess, of contradictions? Being me at home was so completely separate from being me elsewhere, it's amazing I'm not schizophrenic. I was confident, self-assured, often bossy with my brothers and sister, yet I was reticent and shy with adults. I'm sure that grown-ups, with the exception of Mum and Taff, found me distasteful. Neighbours in Fisher's Close eyed me with suspicion, as if expecting me to spit or call abuse at any moment, while I was really a quiet girl, keen to be at peace with people. My teachers treated me as if I was a special needs case, although I was bright enough and got good marks. They always addressed me directly, bending their concerned faces close to my own so that I knew whose teeth were brushed and who hadn't had time to say hallo to Mr Toothbrush. I might have been a deaf child or a foreigner. Such treatment baffled and upset me. Fear of looking as stupid as they thought I was kept me tense, tight, on the alert; I never allowed my mouth to hang open or let my eyes drift out of focus. I know I was a sight (and I was the pick of the bunch since most of my clothes went on down through the other six children) but I still find it depressing that not one teacher ever saw through the tatty exterior.

Children who were not my own brothers and sisters seemed a strange breed to me. I now understand that we were the odd ones out; but at eight, or ten or twelve, my peers were peculiar simply for not being like me. The entire population of the world, or at least of Woking and its surrounding villages, walked in a haze as far as I was concerned, distanced by their lack of perception, their inability to see how wonderful, how glorious we, the children of Victory, actually were. All the same, I was constantly aware of being both special and unseemly: the daughter of the Queen of Magic, half-sister to the Child of the Moon, Gypsy Boy, Son of Satchmo and the little Eskimo lad, not to mention the pixie-faced speedy one and that extraordinary, manicured girl with the Shakespearean name. A lot to live up to. And I headed this troupe, I was the eldest, the leader. It was up to me to steer them from trouble, to teach them right from wrong, to watch over them in cloakrooms where gym kits went missing, in playgrounds where skipping ropes waited to trip them, on buses where they risked having their lunchboxes thrown from the window.

Have you noticed that I make no mention of friends? I had none. I spared no time, made no opportunities for forming friendships; perhaps there was no need. I was one of seven, and then their was my mother, always prepared to listen, to laugh, to help out. Besides, forgive the pathos, but I can't recall anybody making advances, asking if I'd like to sit by them, to walk to assembly in their company, to share a bag of sweets. I know it takes two and, not wanting to be seen to capitulate or conform, I was equally mean with my smiles, my gestures of goodwill. When situations demanded pairing up, for dancing or for the walk to the swimming pool, I was among the last to be chosen, often having to team up with the teacher or with an insipid little boy called Timothy Ross, a creature so nondescript that even when you held his hand you managed to forget he existed. It didn't bother me. I wanted it that way. To join them would have diluted me, or so I believed.

I ought to have seen things differently as I grew up, to have made an effort with my fellow students or the mothers at Bing's play group. I don't think I was aloof, I just never went the extra distance, always turned down offers of drinks or coffees, was always either in a hurry or in love. In my present situation I can see the attraction of close friends. It would be delightful to have a woman, somebody not connected with my family, who knew me well, who cared about my fate. A friend to visit me, to bring frivolous gifts, make-up or magazines, to listen when I spoke of my grief and my new found love. It's a lack I've rarely considered but suddenly it appears as a gaping hole, this friendlessness. Perdita has friends, she always did. I haven't met the present ones, her own smart set, but I expect she's still in touch with Katie, the nice, clean child she befriended at school. They went to Art Club together and invited each other to tea. Lord knows what Katie thought of Perdita's lot, but I know my sister was impressed and embittered by the order of Katie's home.

'Why don't we use napkins?' she asked Mum mournfully. 'And why does Merry make that slurping sound when he eats?'

'It's his way,' Mum explained, 'of showing his appreciation.'

And she presented Perdita with a Man Sized Kleenex in lieu of a serviette.

I shall make some friends when I'm free, get out to evening classes, or join a bridge set. You see, I've no idea how to begin. Of course there's always Liz, but she seems intent on maintaining our agreed silence, and who am I to intrude?

On the way back to my cell today, with your kindly face clear in my mind, I stopped to kick the wall in frustration. The warder handled me roughly and I was glad to feel my muscles burning. If nothing else, pain brings an awareness of life going on regardless. Yesterday, I overheard two of my fellow prisoners as they sighed over a magazine. 'It's not all the crap inside that gets to you,' one said, 'it's thinking of the stuff out there you can't have.'

Too true. Until they let me out of here, I must not only practise restraint, I must also learn the art of doing time.

Do you remember the word you used when telling me how you were enjoying the stories of my family? You said you found them bewitching. An appropriate adjective. I was wondering how my mother would have coped with doing time, and the answer is that she would have bewitched time to make it serve her. Not that she'd have ended up behind bars in the first place; she could make folks forget what they'd seen. Or if, as in my case, the evidence was too glaring to be forgotten, she would talk soothingly until the listener's perspective shifted to her advantage. But supposing she had needed to kill time for some reason; can you believe me when I say she was able to do so?

She could make time stand still. It must be hard to credit and it's almost impossible to prove; although there were eight witnesses with her on the night she achieved this feat. Unfortunately they were all family and may be considered biased. Also, of the eight, my Grandma Editha is no longer living and my brothers Merry and Django would be disregarded as witnesses in any situation. That leaves me, an imprisoned criminal, my other two brothers – Fabian and Samik and my sisters, Zulema and Perdita. From this bunch, Perdita is the only one who could convince even the seriously sceptical that time had stopped. And Perdita might well have chosen to forget the episode. She disapproves of messing about with the status quo, of what happened to her in that non-time, and of my family in general. Perdita is a broker these days, she sells stocks and shares. From the bedlam of The Cornflake House she emerged in a trim suit and crisp white blouse to walk the floors of commerce. As strange a phenomenon as a peacock hatching amongst a clutch of scraggy chickens' eggs. No, Perdita could not be relied on to tell the truth about that timeless night.

Maybe I overestimate your reaction, perhaps it isn't so strange or unbelievable. We change the clocks twice a year, moving our mornings on or our evenings back, and few complain that time cannot be gathered up and herded in such a way. It seems I've begun to think in terms of proving every case, like Valerie. Finding evidence and witnesses to bear me out, when I'm only recounting an event.

Before I tell you what happened, I ought to take you inside The Cornflake House as it was all those years ago and introduce you to its inhabitants one by one. You already know my mother. Then there's Fabian, a troubled teenager at this time, handsome and haunted. He dreams of greatness, longs for fame. He needs to escape, fly the nest and join that gathering of musicians who wait for him. But tonight he's obliged to sit with us, pouting, restless, wasted. Fabian had a tough time in Surrey, being half-caste he was the butt of prejudice and envy. He was every teenage girl's fantasy, except the middle-class white girls of our town weren't supposed to dream in glorious Technicolor.

With Fabian, on one of our sagging sofas, you'll see Zulema. Her skin is not quite as dark as Fabe's, but her eyes and hair are black. At twelve she's already a beauty with graceful movements to match her gentle looks. I used to think she was an angel sent to watch over us; even now I'm not convinced she's an ordinary mortal. Well, mortal maybe, but ordinary, never. As she grew up she became lovelier and more remote. I miss her most of all, but that's the future. Tonight you can feast your eyes on her oval face and share her serenity. I won't blame you for finding yourself drawn to look in her direction.

Sitting all by himself, on his special chair, is Django. By rights, he should look wild, reckless. My mother insists he really did come from the Gypsies. He has brown eyes and twisting hair, but he cuts his locks so short that no curl remains. What is about to happen will have less affect on Django than on the rest of us, because he is already in his evening state of semi-trance. Only the stroke of midnight can wake him. He goes to bed then, counting the stairs, undressing from the feet upwards, brushing his teeth thirty-two times. He reads through his vacuum cleaner catalogues for exactly fifteen minutes and switches his light out at twelve thirty-one. You know, he's the most unlovable boy in the world, but I can't think of him without wanting to grab him in a crushing embrace.

The shining example of cleanliness is Perdita, and pinned to her side, held down by her tidy but forceful hand, is Merry. What a scruff. He's how old? About six I should think. Wonderful face, eyes of polished turquoise, the chin of an apprentice garden gnome. Mind out for Merry, he has a way of landing on people, like a comet.

Grandma Editha has moved in with us now that Eric is dead. She takes the fireside chair, sits so close her knees cook slowly all evening. I swear I sometimes smelt them roasting. Last but not least is Samik, the baby of the family, squashed between Fabian and Zulema. He adores Zulema, who doesn't? And everybody loves him. Right now Samik, at five, is as cuddly as a panda. Sadly he's already suffering from insecurity brought about by teasing and bullying. He's not entirely English, he has a look of Eskimo around the eyes which marks him out for special treatment at school.

All right? Ready to step inside? I'll escort you up the garden path, holding your hand as we pass the caravan and the tree house in the overgrown front garden. Together we can peer through the bubbled glass into the hall. This space glows warmly back at us thanks to red paint and stained-glass lampshades. We go inside and are greeted by a haze of warm, sweet and sour air; musk, incense, dogs, unwashed feet. I allow you a moment to get your bearings; it's a house of contradictions and you might want to focus on a few of these.

What do you notice? The worn but expensive Axminster carpet in bright reds and blues, perhaps. Or the variety of wellingtons that line this Axminstered hall. You might glance down to the kitchen, pink with neon lighting, fitted in best English oak but awash with unwashed pots and pans. We are heading for the door of the cramped, cluttered living room, where I will leave you and yet not move from your side. I have my part to play in the scene you'll watch, but in this instance I can actually be in two places at once. As you stand in the doorway, you'll see them all, two women, three teenagers and four growing children. I'm leaving you now. Yet at the same time I stay and squeeze your hand; don't be alarmed. And please excuse that other me, the overweight, under confident teenager; she has a good heart, under the puppy fat.

It's a story that really should begin 'Once upon a time . . .' because its main concern *is* time. My mother had been experimenting for weeks with the concept of time. Clocks in The Cornflake House had spun backwards, chimed when it was not the hour, jerked their troubled hands forwards as if learning to drive. In those days we children were always in a hurry, late for school, rushing to meet friends, gulping meals. These hiccups in time had been driving us mad. We were used to the unusual but most magic was made to our advantage. On the night that time stopped, we'd been forced to stay in the living room until nearly midnight while our mother hushed us and concentrated hard. We were bored, stiff, fidgety, and then, when she was successful, suddenly stilled.

'I've done it, stopped the clock,' Victory beamed and she waited, momentarily, for our congratulations, before realizing the full implication of her words. She hurried on, 'Sorry, but bear with me, it's taken for ever to achieve this. Not too uncomfy for you, is it?' If it was, we were hardly in a position to say so. 'I think,' she bubbled as she swiped an orange cream from under Grandma's frozen nose, 'that it's the exactness of the hour, or the oh-so-nearly hour, which has made the difference.'

Since I was sitting opposite the fire, facing the narrow mantelpiece on which the clock rested – and I do mean rested – I was the only one who could see and appreciate what my mother meant. It was, as the telephone robot might have said, eleven fifty-nine and fifty-nine seconds, precisely. Midnight hung suspended, frustrated, its throat choked by unchimed bells.

'Ah,' Victory caught my static eye. 'Our Eve can see it, can't you, Love? And can you feel the breeze that holds those hands? The wind of no-change? Course you can.' I couldn't nod or tell my mother how right she was but my hair fluttered obligingly from my face as I stared at the still, silent timepiece. Mum was flushed with success. So much was possible if only there was time to do impossible things. As my mum had pointed out, she who controls time, controls all.

I might have felt more enthusiastic myself if I'd been able to applaud, or at least to speak. Unfortunately for those of us who shared the moment, when time stopped, so did we. Although I was unable now to look around the room, I guessed that petrifaction had taken each of us by surprise. Grandma was almost visible, her fuzzy form sitting stock-still in the corner of my eye. She had her mouth open, having been caught in mid-sentence, and her left hand rested possessively on her precious box of chocolates. The remainder of the family were coloured blurs on the edges of my vision, although I remember I could still smell Merry's infamous feet.

'This side of midnight,' Victory crooned, 'interesting.

You would have thought the magic would wait one second, for the witching hour. Then this would have happened when it was in-between time, neither one day nor the next. What is midnight, after all? Is it today, or tomorrow? Hmm. Seems it prefers to settle for just this side of the obvious. Like myself, of course, exactly like its maker.'

Needless to say I was beginning to wonder how it would end. How long would this last? I wasn't panic-struck because something similar had happened before, at a birthday party, Perdita's, given in honour of her having reached the grand age of seven. The Cornflake House had rocked to the screaming of overexcited children. The kids we'd invited from school and the neighbourhood weren't used to such a glut of freedom, or such a spread of sugary goodies. By the time we'd had our tea, the place was like a home for the hyperactive. More than paper was ripped to shreds as we played Pass The Parcel, and during a game of Shipwrecks, three dear little boys turned the sofa upside down and practically suffocated Sophie Thomas – she'd been sitting on it stuffing her face with what was left of Perdita's birthday cake. When Merry, who had been spinning like a top all afternoon, finally knocked two little visitors over and gleefully threw himself on them, then even Victory had had enough.

'Dead Lions,' she shouted. And Dead Lions we were, every last one of us. Even Merry was stilled, his body at peace in spite of the state of his mind. We must have been the deadest Dead Lions this world has ever seen. We fell like ninepins, stomachs pressed into the carpet. Each of us could see at least a couple of our friends and so we lay numbed, fully able to appreciate how the mighty Kings of Beasts had been felled by one shout.

On that occasion, unlike this, time had not stood still. The hour of the coming of the mothers and fathers approached with speed; and my own mother had no idea how to break the spell.

'Oh dear,' I heard her mutter more than once, 'oh *dear.*' She tried clapping her hands, but the lions remained dead. She put on music and suggested we might like to dance, but our legs stayed still as stones. She even sprinkled pepper on our noses, but simply sneezing was quite beyond us. When the doorbell rang, I felt real panic on my mum's behalf. Here was the first of the parents, come to take their little terrors home . . .

Victory took her time answering that doorbell. Mumbling to herself she shuffled down the hall and let the child-collecting mother in. The two women stood side by side, filling the frame of the living-room door, one gazing fondly, perhaps with admiration for Victory, at the lifeless forms on the floor, the other racking her brains for a solution.

'We've been playing Dead Lions,' Victory explained, unnecessarily. 'We needed a rest, you know, after all the chaos. But now the game is over,' this with more hope than conviction, 'so up you get kids.' No response. 'On your feet now, Living Lions it is.' Magic often responds to opposites and, at long last, just in the nick of time, Living Lions we were.

'Bit of a close call there, eh, Evey?' Mum teased me when the visitors had gone. 'Worried you, did I?' I nodded mutely, my face so close to hers that I could see it in her brown, brown eyes. 'There's always a danger when you let outsiders in, but I don't think any of them noticed.' She was right, the party, discussed next day at school, was 'brilliant', 'smashing', an unqualified success. Nobody even mentioned Dead Lions, it was as if the game had been wiped from their memories altogether.

Well, outsiders weren't a problem when the clock stopped just this side of midnight. At least I guessed it was only us who sat so still in the night. The idea of the entire neighbourhood, perhaps the whole county, stranded as we were was too horrible to contemplate. One thing was certain, nobody was coming to collect or rescue us, so Victory had all the time in the world, and no time whatsoever, in which to reverse our situation.

Typically, as we sat in limbo, Mum decided to put her extra, hard-gained time to good use.

'Might as well make hay . . .' she chirped, and whipped Merry's socks from his feet. On her way to the washing basket, with these rancid tubes dangling between finger and thumb, she passed my line of vision. I heard her filling a basin with water, then the sound of scrubbing. I could smell the soap as she counted Merry's toes in an attempt to make purging into a game.

'Pure perfume,' she sighed. Had I been able to smile, I would have blessed my mother with an appreciative grin.

It was Grandma's turn next.

'These things are bad for you, Mum,' said Victory as she removed the chocolates from Grandma's lap, 'especially the hard ones. Now, you won't mind if I take a liberty? Been bothering me for months and it'll improve your looks no end.' She fished a pair of tweezers from her bag and plucked at Grandma's chin. Three long grey whiskers were flicked from tweezers to waste-paper bin, then Mum stood back, admiring her work. 'Wonderful,' she grinned and patted my grandmother's frail grey head.

Fabian had his fingernails clipped, although Mum was kind enough to leave his 'plectrum' finger alone so that he could still twang his guitar. It took an enormous effort for her to get Django out of his cursed 'Henry' T-shirt. She had to cut both side seams and widen the neck before it would leave his body. It must have been seriously hindering his circulation, making him more constrained than ever. Always the thoughtful one, Mum replaced 'Henry' with another gem. The replacement was several sizes bigger but otherwise identical, a marvellous piece of forethought which she held up before my eyes like a designer at a fashion show.

'You won't know the difference,' she promised Django; but of course he would, which was why, as a safeguard, she popped the small version on the fire – the only thing in the room, apart from herself, that was still moving. While she had the scissors at hand, she brushed Samik's hair 'til it shone as nature had intended, a task that involved a great deal of de-knotting. Then she cut it carefully so that it framed his face but could no longer hide his almond eyes. I only saw the full effect afterwards. It looked stunning.

Next Mum painted Zulema's nails with a layer of that foul stuff which stops the biter from wanting to self-mutilate. I could smell this concoction as I had smelt Merry's feet and the burning T-shirt, and yet again I was filled with admiration for the woman who was always as good as her name.

What, we must all have been wondering, could she do to the already perfect Perdita? Here there was no cleaning or trimming needed. That chestnut hair, brushed a hundred times before bed, was neatly pulled from a face which enjoyed a cleansing, toning, moisturizing routine both night and morning. Those clothes were washed and pressed and fitted like gloves. Her shoes were polished – polished, in The Cornflake House, I ask you – and her teeth flossed. But nothing daunted and never one to leave anybody out, my mother proved once and for all that she was a woman after my own heart. Or I suppose it was my heart that dogged hers so faithfully. She messed Perdita up. Not viciously, as I might have been tempted to do, but just enough to humanize the girl. She undid the top button of Perdita's spotlessly white blouse. She removed the clip and let loose a shampoo-advertiser's dream of shining, bouncy hair. And she removed that cameo brooch which made Perdita look like a member of the lesser aristocracy.

Believe me, I was impressed. I was also, at this point, feeling pretty smug as I imagined I was just fine the way I was. Not perfect in the too well-groomed way of my sister but comfortable and complete. Whereas actually, and I blush to recall this, my mother had been saving the worst 'til last.

'Sorry Darling,' she sighed as she pulled my great sloppy jumper over my head, 'now don't be cross, or embarrassed, but we aren't always exactly as we imagine ourselves. You are blessed, Evey, with a great body. But it's time you appreciated how great it is. You shouldn't be hiding your light . . .' To my horror she was now easing my vest over my head, leaving me exposed to the world, to the fire anyway. 'I bought you this, and believe me you need it.' She produced a bra, holding it up for my inspection before working my arms through the straps. 'It's not even the first, or the second size, Eve. It'll make a whole lot of difference to your life, to the way you walk and hold yourself. I want you to be proud of what you've got, not to keep on pretending they aren't really there. There,' she stood back and congratulated herself, 'that's ever so much better.' My sweater was returned to me, but I knew that if I could, I would have been shivering. Not from cold but from mortification.

The bra, a black satin affair which I later came to love, the anti-nail biting potion and the 'Henry' T-shirt had all appeared from Victory's giant carpet-bag. As I sat uplifted, upholstered almost, I began to understand how much planning had gone into this evening's performance. I imagined my mother in her bed, night after night, not sleeping but dreaming of improving us. Had she found Grandma's whiskers annoying for months, or only weeks? When the rest of us had complained, 'Not the Henry T-shirt again, Django, you look like a stuffed Hoover bag,' had Victory smiled inwardly, knowing that soon she would cut the dreaded thing to ribbons and feed it to the fire? Did the clicking of Fabian's fingernails and those chewed stubs of Zulema's drive her mad? Did we, in fact, each in our way irritate her to death? All credit to her, she never showed any signs of frustration, she'd always been the one, the only one, who absolutely accepted us as we were.

And then I thought how small her alterations had been. When the world mocked us, seemed often to hate us simply for being ourselves, multiracial oddballs, our mother saw us only as her children. If all she wanted to change was our socks or underwear, then the woman deserved a medal.

Once she'd done with me, she sat on the floor, taking her time, a time that existed only for her. She may have thought there would be trouble when we were released, that a period of noise, fighting and tearfulness was bound to follow. She rested as if in meditation, head down, eyes closed, probably calling on something out of the ordinary, even by her standards. Her breathing, a strange mixture of panting, blowing and deep inhalations, finished and we found ourselves able to move again. Amazingly, we weren't angry with her. Not one bit. Time moved on a second and the clock chimed with extra vigour, each ping resounding joyfully through the room until it was no longer midnight but the next morning, and we were late for our beds. One by one we said goodnight and climbed the stairs, or in Grandma's case went through the kitchen to her flat. I don't know about the others, but I guess it was the same for all of us. I felt such a glorious heaviness that I had trouble getting undressed, especially reaching for the hooks of my new bra. I was more than tired, I was compelled to sleep. I remember falling, sweetly and steadily down through my pillows to a place of perfect peace.

I wonder, did you read that story at bedtime? It works for me and I need soothing if ever a person did. Do you see what I'm up to? I'm skating around, trying to kill or to cure time; to drift in memory – avoiding the frustrations of the present.

It'll soon be lights out, time for bed. I am wrapped in sentiment; you are my pillow and my blanket. My hand closes on the little stone frog. I wonder, were you aware of any symbolism when you chose him? You are a small man, Matthew Pritchard, and you hair is going thin, but you are no frog in my eyes. Has nobody ever seen the prince in you before? Have I really stumbled on a man who has been overlooked by the rest of my sex? No, I can't believe no other woman has heard the music in your voice, seen the texture and imagined the warmth of your skin, or lost herself in those gloriously grey eyes. If you were short and fat, instead of being so perfectly proportioned, and if your eyes bulged, which they most certainly don't, then I might assume I was alone in fancying you.

Still, if you believe one kiss might wake the prince in you, what fairy-story hero would my wealth of caresses reveal? Mind you, I'm no princess myself. Only my hair belongs in fairyland and I'll have to cut it soon. As I grow older it will make me seem more witch than princess. I shall miss it, although I took years to appreciate it. As a teenager I used to iron it straight, with only a piece of brown paper between my locks and the heat. Marianne Faithful and Françoise Hardy have a lot to answer for. I thought I looked the bee's knees with my fried hair and my skirt up round my bum. I also had a pair of white plastic boots, thigh high. Boys ran from them in droves – must have thought a couple of giant milk bottles were coming their way.

I hear the warder's approach, doom-laden steps interspersed with the clanging of doors, the turn of the screw. No wonder folks in prison become neurotic, it's like actually having to confront the bogey man, only here he is she and wears a uniform not of ghostly grey but of dull navy blue.

Goodnight Matthew and thank you for the present.

Six

A terrible thing happened to me in the night. I woke to find another body in my bed. My first thought was of the frog. It seemed possible that I had energized and activated him. That the force of my longing, flowing from my hand to his stony being, had brought him to life. Not totally transformed. The thing in my bed had all the damp bonelessness of an amphibian, this was no prince. For a few seconds I lay shivering, anticipating a croak. Then I jumped out of bed and my foot landed on the frog. He'd fallen to the floor as I slept. He was no bigger than before and solid as any pebble. Not magically turned to skin and blood. I swooped like a night owl and plucked him up before darting across my cell to the furthest corner.

As I crouched there squeezing my green friend in my left hand, I knew that if the alien in my bed was no life-sized frog, then it had to be human and from the feel of it, dead human at that. Horrifying possibilities flashed by me. Liz had been unwell, that was why she was tearful. She'd climbed down from the top bunk and died by my side. But as I listened, there it was, that deep breathing; Liz was fast asleep on her bunk.

Perhaps it was the ghost of my mother, my grandmother – worse, of Grandad Eric.

I gathered my panicking thoughts and made them rerun the actual events. I'd been dreaming and had woken bathed in sweat, clammy and aching. Pushing myself to a sitting position, heaving my torso off the mattress, I felt, to my horror, not a frog but a hand under mine. Yes it was a hand, lifeless, limp, as wet to the touch as a drowned man. From my corner I stared at the lumpy bed, waiting for the dead to move.

Slowly my senses began to work again. First my eyes had to become accustomed to the dimness; it's never properly dark, lights always burn beyond the grill in the door. I wondered what goes on, in this or any prison, while we inmates sleep. There were faint voices coming from some-where, I strained to hear them but they slid about like an untuned radio. The whole experience, limp hand, lack of comprehension and not being able to hear clearly, was fright-ening and frustrating. If only I still had my magic, I could have not only listened better but honed in on certain sounds, seen into blocked distances, known much, much more. Soon, at least, I could make out the bed, with the top sheet thrown back to reveal nothing but the bottom sheet, crumpled but uncovered by any body. Then I could smell my own sweat but that was it, there was no hint of death in my nostrils. Lastly my brain began to work. I reasoned that it would have been impossible for a dead person to climb into my bed unaided. And I would have heard, felt and seen anybody putting a body there, beside me. So there wasn't a body in my bed.

But the feeling of a hand under mine had been real

enough and still I shuddered, staying in my corner, cold and shaken. Three of my limbs ached, but my right arm was stinging with fierce pins and needles. I rubbed it gradually back to life, the fizzing alternating between dull and sharp pain as the blood began to flow. I worked from my shoulder downwards, lifting my numb arm, until I reached my hand. And there it was, the limp, boneless object from my bed. Devoid of feeling, my right hand had let my left hand think it was a foreign body, and my brain had believed it too.

Having clapped and slapped my hand back to life, I crawled to the bed where it was chill, damp and lonelier than ever. Not that I'd have welcomed a stiff for a bedfellow but the dream I'd been having before waking so fitfully had been full of life, making me long for voices, movement, company. Staring at the mesh of Liz's bunk, I tried to return to the dream in which I'd been back in that day, long ago, when we had moved into The Cornflake House. The great day when we'd hitched our old caravan to Owen's lorry and rocked our way through England, from the fens to deepest Surrey. In my dream the lorry had become a milk float and our journey, amongst the clanking bottles, had been painfully slow. Not only were we propelled by a single electric battery but we stopped to deliver gold or silver-topped pints to every household on our route. Then there was the orange juice in bottles with shining green tops like beetles in the sun. Merry, just a toddler at that time, made himself sick by drinking milk and orange alternately. Dream vomit, bright yellow with green and carrot-coloured chunks. As the poorly tot hurled himself off the moving float, all arms reached for him and our bodies tumbled after him to land in a sickly heap on the damp verge. I was the last to jump, landing on top of this human pile, with my mother underneath.

'Get off my back,' she cried.

I'd woken up as I rolled over.

After the dream and the dead body incident, I couldn't sleep again. But I did manage to transport myself back to the day the dream had been based on, the day when we'd made the real move. To feel again that wonderful build up of excitement which had highlighted and lengthened the wait. It was late spring and Grandma Editha was boiling with rage and sorrow. She couldn't keep us off her freshly sprouting crops. Our caravan was parked in her garden and although we slept there, on top of each other, we bounced into her house and over the smallholding like hailstones. Our feet must have seemed to be everywhere, but mostly, I imagine, under hers. We weren't dainty children. Nothing was safe in our wake. On the other hand, she was dreading being left alone with only Eric for company. Poor Grandma, she didn't want us to stay and she couldn't bear to think of our leaving.

Grandad hadn't wanted us there in the first place.

'You and your tribe of bastards can camp in a ditch,' he told my mother at the time when she was evicted from the field we used to share with three other families. She ignored him, of course. So he wasn't the least bit sorry when we left. Perhaps he missed us later, the way a ball misses skittles or a dart longs for a bull's-eye. He used a fat round stick as a substitute for his lost leg and since he couldn't kick us, he swung this out at those who were careless enough to venture close. You had to be pretty agile to avoid bruised knees and red shins. This game was his only exercise, that and eating.

Finally the day dawned and we were off on our long-awaited journey. You'd be amazed how much you can fit into one small caravan and an old open-backed lorry. We stacked ourselves high, perching on toys, books, bedding, crockery, and that was only the caravan. Our furniture, such as it was, had been stored in a shed until that day. Now it sat in the lorry, exposed to the sky. Ancient moth-eaten sofas and wormy chairs wobbled under hastily tied ropes and on the very top lay a scratched white table, its legs pointing crudely upwards. We must have looked like refugees.

In my prison bed I lay and smiled to think of the consternation our arrival caused in that exclusive cul-de-sac. What were we? Gypsies? Tinkers? Tramps? A bit of each, all things abominable. The residents' worst nightmares, multiplied by eight and then added to by a number of dogs, cats and rodents. I suppose, if you belong to the middle classes, and if you have invested in a nice, tidy house in a smart location, the arrival of vagabonds in an old, open lorry and a battered caravan is not exactly a welcome sight.

God, it was brilliant to arrive. We were so fed up, having been cramped in that egg of a caravan for hours on end. Except for Fabian who sat like Lord Muck beside Owen in the cab of the lorry. Yes, the rest of us had reached the hair-pulling, head-banging stage, the point where torturing each other was the only way to stay sane.

They had built the houses of our cul-de-sac in an orchard, or on the spot where the orchard had once blossomed. This site was at the bottom of a steep hill and as we descended behind the lorry we were tipped to the front of the caravan and attacked by sliding crockery. Before we could yell at Owen to slow down, he was turning sharp left, swinging us against the windows, then shuddering to a halt. We picked ourselves up, turned around and squashed our faces on the glass to see why we'd stopped.

We had arrived.

It took me a while to understand this, because reality was nothing like my expectations. I'd conjured my own Cornflake House from the artist's impression and my version was prettier than any house I'd ever seen, but only two-dimensional. My imagined house stood, a cardboard cut-out in splendid isolation, in a watercolour meadow. I think there was even a thin, paper Eve gazing wistfully from a bedroom window. The sight I first saw through the caravan window was very different; far from isolated, these dwellings stood almost overlooking each other. In the small sphere of my vision I could see three homes at least, trim as dolls' houses and close enough together to share hammocks. Figures emerged from tidy hallways, people imitating goldfish, mouths opening, closing, dropping open again. Then Owen appeared at the caravan door, 'Reception committee's waiting,' he announced in his finest fen voice.

Dogs escaped instantly, yapping, peeing, heading for the goldfish people. Merry followed them, pushing past Owen, running to catch up, tumbling, screaming and, not being encumbered by a nappy, copying the hounds by pissing against a flowering cherry. The rest of us formed a queue behind our mother, picking up on her anxiety, nervous of meeting our benefactors.

'Which one? Which is ours?'

'Number three,' Mum informed us, 'the one with the flags flying.'

We were shoved back inside, driven in a neat semi-circle, and rearranged right outside our very own Cornflake House.

Like me, you'll have to wait to see the inside of this wonder-home. First you need to know where we were coming from. I described our caravan as an egg because it was cream, oval and had, at Grandma Editha's, rested on a nest of uncut grass. We'd lived elsewhere in our short lives, in flats or bits of shared houses, but our young memories held only dim recollections of solid walls and roofs. To us, until the Day of the Move, home was the caravan, ten by twelve feet of damp, airless mess. There was only really room in there for beds and bedding, everything other than sleep had to be done outside. In summer we ate in the garden, in winter we sat at Grandma's table. We peed in the privy by the side of her square brick house; at least we girls did, the boys watered the crops. Games, including pillow fights, sent us tumbling outside. Unless you sat on the caravan steps, you couldn't even draw a picture without being jogged and distracted.

If we'd previously inhabited an old cottage or a little town house, then the move would have been strange enough. But to zoom up the social ladder, from caravan to Cornflake House, to hatch from thin shell to insulated brick and plaster, this was truly remarkable. It was a little too much for some of us. After all the anticipation, all the excitement, I remember that Zulema and I hung back, timid, overawed, on the caravan step, while the others followed Owen, Pied Piper for a day, whooping, hopping, skipping up the short drive to the front door.

Standing by Zulema in the caravan, I watched my mother shaking hands with a man in a suit, practically dropping a

curtsey to him and his small party of colleagues. Her mouth
moved, presumably she was thanking them for their bound-
less generosity. The man in charge was winded with surprise.
During this, his first encounter with the lucky family, the
poor man aged several years. His eyes did a fair imitation of
Al Jolson, roving from mother to children, from Owen in
his jeans which were held up with string, to Merry who was
hanging semi-naked from a drain pipe. Well. What a shower.
He glanced dubiously at his clipboard, as if it had lied to
him. I suppose Mum's name was written there and my guess
is that he was searching for the word 'alien' in brackets. It
was their own fault, those Cornflake people hadn't bothered
to check us out. We lived so far from London, where the
cornflake company was based, that all communication had
been by post. I bet companies vet folks nowadays, bet you
any money that once this suit-man got back to base he
instigated a new regime for checking on those they may later
have to meet on doorsteps or at posh garages. His colleagues
were pretty stunned too, although one woman – I later
discovered she was the interior designer – couldn't help
smiling to herself. We were decidedly non-U, I'm afraid.
Non-Surrey. It was an embarrassing while before the
Cornflake man recovered his composure. No doubt, in this
interlude, as Merry fell and scratched his bum and Samik
howled for milk, the man considered ways of telling us a
mistake had been made. That we couldn't have this house
and that it would be best for us to clamber back in that hut
on wheels and go away.

There was no escape for him, of course. The home was
ours, fair and square. The photograph they took, of Mum
smiling over the top of Samik's baby head while flags of

many colours flapped round her ears, was later framed and hung in pride of place over the mantelpiece. The suit-man said a few hesitant words of congratulations, then, with a look of undisguised apprehension, he presented Mum with a pair of scissors. The photographer adjusted his tripod and snip, Mum cut the red ribbon. A few hands clapped, a small sound in the great outdoors. Finally, Mum was awarded the key.

We were going to be allowed inside. At last. Even Django, who had a bit of a problem with emotions, was excited. Zulema and I made a slight move, one step towards leaving the old home and getting to the new.

But, as a portent of things to come, before my mother even had time to open her front door, one of our new neighbours strode over to complain. A dog – ours – had shat on his patio. Dino, the dog in question, padded along behind this man, tongue hanging out, tail wagging, looking most relieved. It would have been useless to argue with that.

'It'll be cleared up by the time you get back,' Mum promised.

'Is that it?' our neighbour growled, obviously unimpressed by this magical offering. 'Aren't you even going to say you're sorry?'

'Of course I'm sorry. I wouldn't be clearing it up if I wasn't.'

At this point, Django, who had been staring at the newcomer, tugged the man's sleeve. Reluctantly the man looked down, his face stiff with disapproval of my little brother.

'You have a bogey,' Django told him, 'you should wipe your nose, it's disgusting.'

Owen laughed and patted Django on the back. 'Check mate,' he said.

There was more than a moment's silence and even at a distance, I understood that from this point of impasse things might go one of two ways. In terms of social blunders, we were equal, and we were neighbours. The man might find a hanky, use it, laugh too, shake hands and be friends. Or he might glare, stamp and become a sworn enemy. I hoped for the hanky, but was disappointed. This was a stamping, glaring man. His scowl encompassed my family, Owen, and the reception committee; but suit-man and co. met his gaze with well-rehearsed smiles which sent him thumping back to his soiled patio.

Mum turned to Zulema and me. 'Come on girls,' she begged, 'you should be here for this.' We hung back, reluctant to join an atmosphere which had turned sour. Over the years I've imagined that I heard my mother speak again, but I think she was silent. I don't know; she might have said, as she put the key to the door, 'I wish Taff was here.' Even if she didn't speak aloud, she must have thought it, because there was a sudden honking of car horns, spluttering of engines, calling of excited voices; and there was Taff, all hair and grin, leaping from an open-topped sports car. She held a bottle of champagne in each hand and although several young men were emerging from her convoy, she eyed suit-man and shouted, 'Extra rations, you're brilliant you are, Vic.' It was party time.

Thinking about it, I believe Taff was the first to step inside The Cornflake House. Mum turned the key, held back the door and Taff's stilettos sank into the newly fitted Axminster. By the time Zulema and I crept in, Taff was in full swing, swigging straight from the bottle, filling the empty house with 'oohhs', and 'just get a load of this, Vic'.

I saw a lot of floor, some banisters, and many adult knees as I stole from room to room. There wasn't much else to see, empty houses are sorry places, especially when decorated entirely in a wan blue. This colour was, next to having to contend with Taff, my greatest disappointment. I remembered the description Mum and I had hung over, the words I'd read to her so often '. . . *Enjoying a quiet, orchard setting, your three-bedroomed Dream House will have a modern, fully fitted kitchen complete with washing machine, refrigerator and stainless-steel sink unit. You will be able to relax in your pale turquoise bathroom before slipping into bed in the luxurious master bedroom. The walls will have been painted in Duck Egg Blue and the floors will be fitted with a carpet of your choice.*' Well, if this was Duck Egg Blue they'd been feeding the ducks the wrong stuff. I looked at the bright, positively garish carpet.

'What'll it be, Evey?' Mum'd asked when we went to see Mr Pollard who ordered rugs and lengths of carpet for those who came to feel their way through his stack of hairy books. At least the Axminster was all it was meant to be.

'Just needs a lick of paint,' Mum made me jump, as she so often did when reading my thoughts. She'd sneaked up behind me to admire the luxurious master bedroom, and with her arm over my shoulder I felt, at last, that what was happening was real. Or was it? It was down to her magic, our being there, our owning the place. But . . . one snap of her fingers would banish the house to oblivion.

She never did snap her fingers to break the spell. We lived in our Cornflake House because my mother believed it was meant to be. Had destiny intended us to stay in our caravan, then Mum wouldn't have bought the box of cornflakes in the first place. The artist's impression of a Dream House on the back of that box, the invitation to try her luck, wouldn't have caught her eye, enticing her to have a go at the competition. What's more, I don't believe Mum would have entered the competition unless she knew, without any doubt, that she would win. She was more than lucky. Nobody played cards with Mum more than once. Dice fell into any pattern she wished and we kids knew better than to invite her to play games of chance with us. I remember one time when Zulema and I were playing Pick-A-Stick, you know, that game where you drop a stack of coloured sticks in a tight formation and have to take them one by one without moving any of the others. Those bits of wood remained still in impossible situations for Mum, until we were forced to accuse her of cheating. 'Can't help it,' she shrugged, and I don't suppose she could.

When Bingo became popular she used it as a method of getting us a bit of extra cash. She won raffles all the time and being so fatalistic she felt obliged to keep the prizes whether she wanted them or not. Of course a house is a little different from the average raffle prize, you can stuff a box of hankies or some unwanted soaps in a drawer and forget about them, but a house . . . Still, I'm almost certain she did want this particular prize.

You had to say which 'luxuries' were best, in our competition for the house, put in order of preference things we'd never seen before. It was boom time, women, having worked through the war, were supposed to be lusting after labour-saving gadgets. These delights would seem primitive to us now, the 'super-twin' washing machine, which included 'Spin

Drying!', was the size of a small garden shed, but each item was miraculously modern then. We put the Dishmaster fairly low on our list, it being hard to cope with the idea of a machine doing our mountains of washing-up, but the Kenwood Chef, billed as 'your servant in the kitchen' sounded just the job. And as I say, Mum knew only too well that she was getting it exactly right. There was a tie-breaker to finish in no more than ten words . . . 'I eat my cornflakes every morning because . . .' We mulled this over for a while, until Mum came up with; 'all year round, there's sunshine in every crispy, crunchy bowlful.' Simple, but effective; nobody had ever equated cereal with the weather before.

Those who doubt the existence of magic should have been there, in that sleepy Lincolnshire village when Mum and I posted our entry. I swear the envelope floated down that post-box. And if that wasn't convincing enough, they should have seen our faces when we opened the reply. Mum might have known she'd win, and I had my suspicions, but the rest of them could hardly take it in.

'A *house*?'

'Yes, a whole house.'

'We won a house? By eating cornflakes?'

'And doing a quiz thing, yes.'

'A house? Like Grandma's?'

'Umm, but modern, with an indoor toilet and stuff.'

'Will we have to give it back?'

'Will we have to share it?'

'Will we have our own rooms?'

'No; no; and of course not. It's a house, not a Grand Hotel. It's got three bedrooms, not eight.' But still, three bedrooms, detached, with gardens front and rear – and all for next to nothing, for eating one box of cornflakes instead of the gooey porridge Grandma usually dished up. My brothers and sisters made me read the glorious news over and over '... *delighted to tell you / please confirm by return of post / we look forward to hearing which carpets you have chosen,*' and yet again I read the phrase, '*your very own Dream Home*'. Those five words must have been repeated hundreds of times. The smallholding might have been on a cloud, the air was light with dreams come true.

It seemed, after all, that there was a God. And He was, to quote the hymn, good, good, good, and He smiled, unlike most adults, benevolently down on us. A vast, charismatic figure of the heavens who could change fortunes with a wink of his eye. In my imagination, this deity was a cross between the standard bearded father figure and Hughie Green.

But have you ever considered that expression; dreams come true? Today, with the arrival of the national lottery, there are new millionaires every week, twice weekly in fact. According to reports, instant wealth can bring pleasure and pain in equal measures. In our dreams we omit the pain, naturally enough. Sun shines on us as we drive gleaming convertibles, champagne corks pop, fountains play in the large, well-kept gardens of these dreams. But imagine great riches actually falling on your head, sudden as death. Everything would need to change. Deceits would have to be practised, moves made. We'd discover a fresh set of worries. Where would we be made welcome, where would we belong? I have no answers so I'm grateful to be the child of a wise woman. My mother had the ability to harness chance. For all I know she may have looked down that road and seen a future in which we had limitless funds. Maybe she foresaw one child after another going off the rails, taking drugs, killing themselves in fast cars. Maybe. For reasons best known to herself, she rationed her good fortune, tempered any greed she may have experienced. If she'd wanted to, she could have picked six numbers from forty-nine as easily as you might select a decent wine in an off-licence; but she believed in effort, knew the delight in spending one's own hard-earned wages; understood that some dreams are best left unfulfilled.

Yet she won us The Cornflake House, because we were out-growing our caravan, because she thought that, having only the one parent, we deserved at least the stability of bricks and mortar. Did other families ever seriously consider the possibility of winning one of those prize houses? Did people transport themselves, whilst munching their breakfasts, into the back-of-box world created by an artist who was only allowed to use three colours? I mean I really don't know how carried away with fantasy folks get, when there is only a remote chance of winning – and statistics to prove exactly how remote that chance is. But if they did follow through that dream scenario, I suspect they may have found themselves wondering if winning a home was what they really wanted. Home; an emotive word, conjuring, for most of us, an image of our chosen haven. Does anybody who hasn't won a major, life-changing prize ever realize the stigma of winning? Perhaps the truth is that there are no winners; you are vomited out of one class without hope of being accepted by another. Those who own property are top of the pile, those who rent still have aspirations, ambitions, but those who get their houses by chance have no say and no status. There you have it, do you see? We won and we

were grateful; but in different circumstances we might have
been even more fortunate. We might have been able to
choose where we lived. Supposedly, the essential things in a
person's life are their relationships with other people and
their relationship with their surroundings. Take one family
of vagabonds, move them across England from secluded
Lincolnshire smallholding to select Surrey cul-de-sac, and
stand back, wait for the fireworks.

On our first night as homeowners, while the party raged
and neighbours popped by to complain about the noise,
Mum sensed my feeling of anti-climax. She made me a fizzy
drink which I imagine was three parts champagne and one
of orange squash and which restored in me a feeling of
excitement and well-being. So, drunk as the rest of them,
I sailed through the evening, hardly noticing the gradual
way in which the rooms filled with furniture. Having taken
a nip or two, to help them recover from the shock, even
the cornflake manufacturer's representatives helped out. I
remember being asked to hold the suit-man's jacket while
he helped Owen with a sofa. In fact some of the cornflake
people were still there, hanging over various chairs, when
we kids came charging down the stairs the next morning.

The party, Dino and Merry's toilet habits and the sight
of the poor caravan rocking to the strains of Taff and her
current choice of lover, set the seal on our relationship with
the inhabitants of Fisher's Close, the cul-de-sac where The
Cornflake House was built. Why the place was called Fisher's
Close when it was on the site of an orchard, I never could
fathom. I suppose the builder must have been a Mr Fisher,
or a man who fished. The other home owners chose more
appropriate names, Cherry Tree, Apple Orchard, Damson

House. (There seems to have been some confusion as to what fruit had been grown there before the land spurted those little dream homes.) Had we been accepted, welcomed, my mother might have decided on Pear Blossom or the like for our house. But since we were met with resentment and distaste, she painted our legend on a large piece of wood, in letters red as blood, and nailed this sign to a post on our front lawn. She used a sledgehammer on the post, staking respectability through its heart. 'The Cornflake House' sign stood up to all weathers and was repainted each year so that it might shine as a constant reminder.

I ought to point out how very select the area around Fisher's Close happens to be. Across the narrow road beyond the close lies a golf course, open only to those with large bank balances and the correct outfits. The course is serene, paint-box green with puddles of pale yellow sand. It's bordered by the 'rough', a stretch of bracken and shrubs which is a paradise for wildlife and for kids playing Hide and Seek or Cowboys and Indians. Further afield the land is a pleasing patchwork of meadows and copses, dotted with small ponds. The houses there are grand affairs, borrowing styles from many countries and ages, but each hidden discretely beyond drives of laurel or rhododendrons. A walk or bike ride down the leafy lanes of this part of Surrey leaves you with the impression of distant chimneys, half glimpsed tennis courts, a dash or two of turquoise from a far swimming pool. A couple of miles down the road you come to the country's largest cemetery. Acres of graves and tombs are separated by a maze of paths. Quite a playground, for children with a suitable sense of the macabre. Zulema was especially fond of this place, begging me to follow her there on our old bikes, persuading me to play refugees searching for lost families, mothers hunting for the graves of tiny infants, jolly games like that.

For the seriously energetic, beyond the vast cemetery, is a heath, a tangled prickly expanse, not to be explored without a bag of provisions and a compass. After a rare fight with my mother I once ran away, empty-handed, to this heath and hid in a dip. I hoped I would be found, hugged, forgiven and led home. In silence I grew colder and more frightened as darkness threatened. At dusk I clambered out of my pit and raced towards the sound of traffic. A man in a Jaguar gave me a lift. The journey, which had taken hours on foot, was over in five minutes; the row was over too, thank God.

Into this rich man's paradise our family fell like fleas on velvet.

We were lucky to have Owen helping us with the move. Apart from the obvious benefit of his biceps, having a man by Mum's side as we arrived made us seem slightly less outlandish. We must have looked like a complete family, large but not without the correct balance of adults. On the other hand you wouldn't have needed a degree in genetics to see that Owen was not father to many of us. He was a bristly man. I supposed he did shave, but his cheek could make a child's skin sting for hours. We were always hungry for male company. Being fatherless we attached ourselves to Owen, bristles and all, like leeches. He loved the attention we gave him, but best of all, he loved Victory. As usual, this love was not returned. I expect Owen harboured hopes of fathering an eighth child; but my mother was so into the mystical that seven was the number she had chosen and seven we were to stay.

Owen seemed to us to have appeared from nowhere, but I suppose my mother picked him up on one of her nights out. She still went out on the town with Taff while we were living at Editha's smallholding. I remember the scent of violets and the two of them giggling as they tried on each other's lipstick. Taff was a dazzling blonde with a sexy, floppy fringe at that time. She tended to go for pinks, as shocking as possible. My mother looked best in crimson. Every time I smelt that perfume and saw those make-up bags open, my heart would sink. Being left out is bad enough but being left in charge of a tribe like ours, knowing that Fabian would bully me and Merry would crash into me all night . . . well it wasn't my idea of fun. I'm ashamed now, of my long, sulky face. My mother deserved a break if ever anybody did.

There was usually an Owen, or a Pete or a Dave in my mother's life. They had little joy with her, after – I imagine – the initial bliss of sexual conquest. She tired of them instantly, as if the act of sex was an end in itself. Owen stayed the first night with us in The Cornflake House but he and his lorry vanished in a cloud of exhaust the next morning. He'd lasted longer than most. Looking back, I honestly think my mother kept him hanging around while she arranged the move simply because he had a lorry. After Owen there were no others. Not in the house anyway. Mum still dabbed her neck with violet scent and went out when Taff came to stay, but she never brought a man home.

Anyway, back to our first days in our shining new house. Seven children of mixed origins and a mother who looked like a Gypsy fortune-teller. I wonder who was the most stunned? Us at finding ourselves so socially elevated, or our neighbours who must have believed the god of housing estates was playing a bad joke on them?

I think the position of our caravan was the last straw. Before he left, and after Taff was through with it, Owen towed it on to the front lawn, stuck a pile of bricks under the tow bar and threw open the door to air the old heap. And there it rested, never more to sway down the lanes of England. Demoted from home to playhouse over night. It didn't go to waste; bears and dolls lived there for years, rigid in front of plates of paper food. Wounded mice and wild rabbits hid or were hidden there, away from the cats and dogs. Almost every one of us children buried diaries and notes inside the built-in beds. My mother wasn't a great believer in punishment, but she would sometimes ask offending children if it might not be a good idea for them to spend a while in the caravan, cooling off. We went willingly; space all to ourselves was considered a prize.

I believe it will still be moored there, our egg-house, looking more incongruous than ever. It stood out, as if a dinosaur had laid it, amongst the neat, communal front gardens. The caravan represented our old life, the days before we reached The Cornflake House, when we ran even wilder and met no opposition, knew no prejudice. We never outgrew its confines. One by one, as adolescence bit us, we found it an invaluable refuge. The ideal place to try out new make-up or to squeeze spots in private. Perfect for late-night goodbyes, an oasis of softness in a prickly world, tailor-made for snogging. I had my first French kiss in the caravan, my tongue tentatively exploring the roof of Brian Holder's mouth while persistent rain drenched less fortunate lovers.

If my name wasn't worse than mud in Fisher's Close, I would take you there, Matthew, on my first night of freedom and teach you the true meaning of rocking around the clock.

Seven

I'm in the toilet, the washroom, having a wash, only face
and hands. We get baths twice weekly and then I dip my
head under the water and let my hair float free. Other than
that I wash each evening. This is evening and I'm soaping
my palms, a soothing action learnt in early childhood and
practised daily throughout my life. I'm remembering, as
usual, the little turquoise bathroom of The Cornflake House
and how we'd fight for a few moments' privacy there,
amongst the seashells and rather smelly flannels. There was
always somebody huffing on the landing outside, impatient
for their turn. It strikes me as odd that I've got this place to
myself, it's more often a case of standing in a line, touching
elbows with other women as they rinse the day's dirt from
their faces. There's an eerie moment when I consider my
solitude in this busy place more than odd, but only a
moment, for the door bursts open and I have company.

There isn't time to count them, or to do anything other
than register the fact that this is no friendly social call. I see
a snarl in blurry close-up, as if I am a camera with an
unadjusted lens. I see the snarl, then the floor comes up to
meet me and in my open, protesting mouth is a foot, and in

my hair is a hand, screwing its way through, twisting and pulling until it has me by the scalp. Shock has not yet given way to pain, I notice that the tap is still running and that my hands are too soapy to be of use. The floor is cold, wet, and a little bloody. Also it's littered with hostile feet. Something hits my back, winding me again, sending alarm signals from screaming spinal cord to slowly adjusting brain. I am being attacked.

Now I'm terrified. I try to curl up like a foetus, to give them less area to attack, to appear headless. But they find me again, hate me more than ever, hit me harder. This time the blows take out the centre of my face, ridding me of a mouth and a nose with well-aimed punches. I have no features now, just a throbbing mess of offal under my forehead. The back of my skull hits the floor a second time, and a kick finds my left breast which erupts instantly in pain. They are saying things, spitting words down on me, hateful, untrue accusations that arrive on my pulped face in gobs. Through my tears I can see a tooth, not white but pink with saliva and blood, a few inches from my left arm. I reach for it, my hand travelling through a pair of stocky legs to make the rescue. Then a foot comes down hard on my fingers and I make a sound that is an ending in itself. Not groan or scream, it's more of a siren. It frightens them; it scares me too. Muttering, my attackers turn and leave.

From my spot on the floor I can see the underside of the porcelain basins. Not too clean, considering there's a toilet duty every day. There are lumps of gum stuck to some of them. I might be able to reach a rim, to haul myself up, but my arms are jelly. Besides there are mirrors up above. No it's better here, safer here. The floor doesn't feel cold anymore, although I'm shivering now, but that's shock, isn't it? Not cold, not dead, just shaken to the core. My wounds are beginning to make themselves felt, the sharp pain in my back, the throb of my breast, the crushing ache in my hand. As for my face . . . I start to move my good fingers tentatively towards my mouth, but think better of it, afraid of finding only a hole filled with liquid. Of course I'm crying and there is comfort in these tears, I let them wash the wounds I can't lick. They ooze from between puffed eyelids, flowing with ease, like urine from a bed-wetting child. It would be wise to call for help but that siren-sound has finished me, the only noise I can offer is snivelling, self-pitying sobs.

'I want my mummy,' I think, and it makes me smile. At least the corner of what was my mouth moves and I taste blood in my throat. Now I remember, I've been here before, down on the floor with a thick tongue and swollen eyes. Am I dreaming or remembering? Is there that great a difference? My poor eyes close, my head spins recklessly.

I'm fourteen again and it hurts. I'm sorry for myself and sorry I disobeyed Mum. I ought to be at home, looking after the others. I said I'd stay while she nipped up to London, I promised. Now look what you've done, silly girl. And you can stop saying that, repeating that as if it will make everything all right. They'll think the blow has knocked the sense out of you.

'I am Eve, the first born. I am Eve, the first born.'

'What's that, Love? Never you mind now, we'll soon get you sorted.' It's a man, his face is close to mine. I think he's a Nazi, there's a suspicious looking badge on his black jacket. Am I dying? Maybe this is hell, peopled not with devils but with fascists. There are people all over the ground, some with injuries, some sitting stunned. The place is foggy, full of smoke. A child is crying nearby and somewhere a man is groaning. I feel very sick so I lie back and think of home, screwing up my eyes to concentrate on the picture of Mum that's gradually coming into focus.

'Evey, Evey, what are you doing here? What happened to you?'

'Mum?' Yes, it's my mum, nobody else smells that good, feels that wonderful, sounds so reassuring. We are hugging, her kneeling, me sitting up in her arms. Rocking together on the dirty concrete floor of the station, in the pigeon shit. It'll be all right now, Mum's here. She asks me, 'Can you walk?' I nod and my head aches as it moves. My legs feel fine, wobbly but uninjured. The Nazi isn't sure, he offers me a hand which I don't take as he tells Mum he thinks I should stay still a bit longer. Long enough for him to fetch the Book Of Registration, I suppose. No way, wobbly legs or no, I'm out of here.

We are on the train, Mum and I. Going back to Woking through the suburbs. I have a blinding headache, stinging eyes and a great happy grin. I lean on my mother as the train shudders us homewards.

'I saw you in the air,' I tell Mum, 'a second before I was blown-up, I caught a glimpse of you above me. You were waving your arms about.'

'Mmm,' she nods, 'trying to get the buggers to listen, in vain, of course. I was behind glass, Evey, not floating magically over your head. I was in the Station Master's office. He's got a good view from there, long windows looking down on everything. I thought if I held him, just lightly touched his arm say, that he'd see what I saw. Danger coming, that's what I saw. But he pulled away. Thought I was batty. Too late now. Lucky that St John's man found you, and a good thing you called for me.' Had I called? In my head I had, I suppose.

My head is clearing. I have a past as well as this sore present. Only this morning Mum told me she'd have to go out, got to get to London, she said. I was meant to stay and look after the other kids but I couldn't. She was so het-up, it frightened me. I thought they'd be fine with Fabian and Zulema. Why did it always have to be me who mothered them at such times?

'I followed you,' I tell her, 'all the way to Waterloo.'

'You shouldn't have. You might've been killed.'

'Not with you around,' and I cuddle up closer. We are silent for a while. The landscape is opening out now, more green than grey.

Then she speaks again.

'I wasn't much use today, not to you or anybody. Oh, I saw it coming, felt the vibrations and heard the screams' – I shudder at this – 'but I don't know why I bothered. People didn't listen, they never do.' And then I remember that I'd also known the explosion was coming, but only a few seconds before it happened. I'd stood amongst the crowds trying to make sense of the inexplicable panic in my head and just before the bomb went off I'd run to a wall and flattened myself against it. That explained why my face was hit by bits of flying debris. I should have found a bench and hidden under it. Next time, I think, I'll know better. And I begin to cry, snuggled in my mother's armpit, because there might not have been the chance of a next time. I might have been killed. So might she; and she knew the risk she was taking.

I swallow blood, my lip is badly cut, and I swear by every drop of blood in my body to take better care of my mother from now on.

But how can I care for her now that she's dead?

'Leave me,' I tell him, thinking it's the St John's man again, trying to move me so Mum won't be able to find me, 'leave me here.' Of course it's not him, it's a member of the prison staff lifting me from my now familiar patch of floor to lead me to the sickbay.

Here is the doctor, a woman with a long face and hands like a jellyfish, covered in cream latex. She seems a bit flustered, for a professional. Maybe she'd have liked to have trained as a hairdresser, but had ambitious, pushy parents. No, it appears to be me who's unnerving her. Do I look that bad? Obviously I do. She checks for broken bones, tests my reflexes, covers me in ointments, and the whole examination is done with an air of distaste. Clearly she'd rather be somewhere else; even through the gloves her hands cringe from touching me. I understand. She longs to be curing just your common or garden murderer. She's heard the accusations then, and believes them.

Now I'm resting in a bed, not in my cell but in a quiet cubicle, under fresh sheets. I ache all over, even my toenails are tender. Also it feels as if my innards are composed entirely of liquid; perhaps I'm haemorrhaging. I would call the doctor back but her distaste clings bitterly to my tongue, leaving me speechless. I ought, after such an outburst of hatred, to be able to deal with a little antipathy. Now it comes rushing back to me, the venom with which I was attacked. To be hated so passionately, it winds you for ever. I've never hurt anyone. Never killed so much as an insect, knowingly. Yet those women, who must have sat near me at mealtimes, passed by me in corridors, maybe even smiled at me in that very toilet, crushed me to within an inch of my life. I can sense the build up of violence now, now that it's too late. One word leading to another, Chinese whispers turning to spit, poisoned glances. Are they a different breed from me? We're all prisoners, shouldn't we share a common pain? Ah but I ignored them, kept myself apart, because of grief and love I may have given the impression of thinking myself too good for them. I didn't communicate with my fellow inmates. Except for that one time when I had a confrontation about biscuits, making an enemy by refusing to give in. Is that what filled them with self-righteousness? I mean I know they hate me for what they believe to be my crime, but it had to begin somewhere. There must have been a seed, venom grows slowly in dark corners, it doesn't arrive fully fledged.

Best not to dwell on it. Better to think back to the past, beyond the loathing in the toilet and the distaste in the sickbay. I've met that distaste before, first and second hand; I guess we all have. My mother told me, in an attempt to demonstrate how desirable Taff used to be, about the night two young men nearly killed each other for love – although it sounded a lot like lust to me. It was in the early fifties, excessive days by all accounts when, because sugar and sex were no longer rationed, life was sweet and spicy. The two friends were working together, serving meals in a canteen for the bus drivers and conductors of Lincoln.

'We wore green headscarves to keep our hair off the food, and flowery wraparound pinnies, made us look like upside-down gardens,' Mum recalled, 'but in the evenings we became exotic birds. There were the long promised nylons to make our legs shimmer and shoes had deviated from frumpy to flimsy, from solid round toes to dangerous points. Waists were all the rage and we were lucky there. Working in a canteen, sliding eggs from greasy pans all day, put us off meals. We lived on bananas, oranges and tinned pineapple, the things we'd missed during the war, and we could squeeze ourselves into the tightest, widest belts.'

I expect the violet perfume and bright lipsticks were used unsparingly. I've seen photographs of them arm in arm, Taff a few inches taller than Victory and with longer, fairer hair. Both are glowing with anticipation. It was a double date, set up by Taff who was, for once, uncertain of her man. Mostly they dated bus drivers and conductors, enjoying, after a film or a dance, the luxury of plush seats, upstairs or down, to themselves in the dark, deserted depot. But this time they were going out with a taxi-driver called Mac who had strayed into their canteen and stolen Taff from under the nose of her current beau. Taxi-drivers were a bit classier, or so Taff thought, although this one had a shifty look. She agreed only to a double date.

'I'll bring me brother,' Mac had winked at Mum. 'He likes 'em dark and stormy.'

'What's his name?' Mum thought that names contained the essence of people.

'Kenneth,' Mac said, his eyes focused on Taff's floral figure. Kenneth sounded a solid, dependable name. The women consented to meet the brothers outside the Odeon, Friday, at seven sharp.

'They dragged us straight to the back row,' Mum told me, 'no ifs or buts. I was on the end, by the aisle. Well, I thought, at least I'll be able to grab an ice-cream in the interval, or to make a quick exit. Kenneth sat between me and Taff, fidgeting, eating boiled sweets without offering them round, sniffing, crossing and uncrossing his legs. He was most unlike his name, small and oily. I didn't fancy him one bit, and the feeling was mutual, I could tell. Fine by me. I settled down to watch the film as best I could, considering I was next to an eel. To be honest, Eve, I didn't see that one coming. I was disengaged, sort of, from the vibrations, lost in a black and white world of soppy American romance. I knew Mac was well away with Taff, that was only to be expected, other than that I was unaware of my surroundings.'

They were thrown out, all four of them. A fight began when Kenneth's hand, exploring Taff's left leg, met Mac's hand, exploring Taff's right leg, somewhere between her thighs. The air turned blue. As the manly film star whispered soft words of love, the flesh and blood men swore obscenities at each other and eventually at Taff who tried to separate them by swinging her handbag from groin to groin. My mother told me she was almost hysterical with glee and responding to a demon in her guts, she took off one of her wonderful pointed shoes and prodded Kenneth in the buttocks with the heel of this fashion item. All around them couples were giving themselves stiff necks turning to shout for peace. It took the manager, an elderly, timid man, both usherettes and the projectionist, to disentangle the four fighters and evict them from the building. During the fracas the reel of film ended and the audience shouted and booed at the poor man who had left his hideaway to help out so gallantly.

They none of them saw the blood, because of the street lighting and their eyes adjusting from the cinema. Taff was cursing the fellows, her stockings were laddered and her handbag hung by a broken strap.

'Bloody fools,' she told them, 'great pair of bloody babes, fighting like schoolboys.'

Then, at last, my mother's intuition returned. Sensing that Mac was about to make a getaway, she grabbed him by the back of his mohair jacket and he found himself pinned to the spot. Next, Kenneth let out a groan and fell flat on his face. My mother was seriously worried for a second, imagining her heels had done the damage, but the blood, and there was quite a pool of this, was seeping from his front, oozing under his flattened belly.

'Get an ambulance,' she ordered Taff. She only released Mac once the doors of this emergency vehicle were open and he'd climbed inside.

It seems, like his namesake in the song, Mac had been carrying a knife. I don't know which came first, Taff's date or the record, but I do know that Mac wasn't back in town for quite a while. What struck Mum was the way they were all shunned by the authorities. It was fair enough to expect police, doctors and nurses to handle Mac roughly, to dismiss his complaints of pains and cracked ribs, but they were equally full of condemnation for Kenneth and the women. Taff bears a scar to this day, a silver line across her right hand which she got when she clashed with Mac as he aimed for Kenneth's guts. It was some time before this was stitched and then it wasn't neatly done.

A bedtime story. It might be bedtime, I have no idea. Whatever the hour, here I lie, telling myself stories when . . .

what should I be doing? Considering my plight, I suppose. But I refuse to reflect on the words used as weapons by my attackers. All right, I've committed an exceptional crime, but then I come from an exceptional family. Besides, they're wrong, I'm not the fiend they make me out to be. I'm not about to be tried for that, not for anything so dreadful. I wish it was over, much as I dread the trial, I want the whole business behind me. If I could scream, I might drown the accusations.

There are pale neon lights burning beyond the door, giving the illusion of evening, an insipid sunset. Whether or not it is night, I'm in no fit state to sleep. If I close my eyes, feet kick at my face again, or fists fly in my direction. I'll lie here, awake, alone with my memories and thoughts for days and days. Three monkeys rolled into one, not listening or speaking, and seeing not a soul.

Eight

The best laid plans ... Even after I'd been dismissed and returned to my cell, where I managed not to look Liz in the eye but merely to keep my sore head down, I meant to stick to my plan of seeing no visitors. This includes you, Matthew. I'm not proud of my newly arranged face. But I had to meet with Valerie. The trial date approaches and she will insist on talking to me, although I try not to hear because what she suggests is absurd.

To add to my distress, I had a visit from Merry and his carer. I wasn't going to see them either but they'd come a long way and I was told Merry was in a state – when is he ever not? – so I gave in and limped to greet them. It was a mistake. My body hadn't finished trembling; I wasn't ready to be confronted by those goggling eyes or that vacant, innocent face. We hugged and cried, Merry weeping in imitation. Other prisoners and their visitors stared open-mouthed at my brother but he was oblivious, concentrating on his planned speech:

'Mum's ... dead,' he told me.

I nodded.

'You sad?'

'Yes Merry, I'm sad. Are you?'

'Oooh yes.' He pushed his mouth into what he thought might be an appropriate shape. His carer, a kind, heavily tattooed man called Jim, held Merry's arm with exactly the right blend of force and sympathy. He'd sensed that Merry was about to start jumping on the spot.

'He's been pretty good,' Jim told me, 'until last week.' Since I didn't understand the implication, he explained, 'Time for his visit home. He looks forward to it, you see.'

'Oh, Merry,' and fresh tears oozed from my puffball eyes. Jim studied his booted feet. Merry studied me.

Guilt came with all the force my assailants had used, hitting me where it already hurt. The importance of home in Merry's cheerful and uncomplicated world hadn't occurred to me before. He was in a Home, well fed, constantly entertained, cared for, and I'd not thought of him looking forward to visiting me and Mum. Until then I would've said that Merry was incapable of looking forward to anything. He seemed to live entirely in his own busy present. But of course he has a memory, a limited, more selective memory than most of us; I could see that if he had a past he might also have sometimes given thought to a future.

This fresh onslaught of guilt was just what I didn't need with my body bruised and my mind already shuddering in my skull. Much of my childhood had been spent worrying over Merry, tugging him from trouble, making excuses for his behaviour, defending him. Whatever I did for him, I invariably failed because then as now I couldn't solve the essential problem, which was Merry himself. Of all my brothers and sisters Merry was the one who could never be guided, who wouldn't sit on a knee and listen while Mum or I explained the ways of the world. Well, only reincarnation or similar miracles would help my brother now, or me for that matter.

I wasn't surprised by his sorrow because I'd seen him sad before. He has little idea how to express his feelings but he does feel, if only fleetingly. It was Merry who instigated our Day of Deep Sadness, when he was still quite a little boy.

It was a Sunday and even though there was only one family in Fisher's Close who actually went to church, revving their Austin pointedly to ensure we Philistines appreciated their piety, all residents but us treated the day as holy. On the Sabbath one might water one's roses, but gently with the hose pointing to heaven. One could bring forth sponge and bucket and wash one's motor car but the rubbing and rinsing must be done languidly, as that woman washed Jesus' feet in the bible. Meat must be eaten, with roast potatoes and two veg, the whole covered in smooth Bisto, at one to one-thirty. To sit down to this feast before such time, or indeed to arrive late for it, as did some wicked men who went for a drink at the Jolly Farmer first, was a sin which could only be absolved by an afternoon reclining in a Parker-Knoll chair. God knows how the middle-class British Sunday evolved; and He may know, but I bet it still baffles Him.

We, of course, were Pagans. To us Sunday was a non-school, no-shops-open kind of day during which we must make our own entertainment. It was the day for discovering why our bikes wobbled, or for finding out exactly what was stuck between the wheels of our roller skates. On Sundays we exercised the dogs, throwing sticks and balls across the garden, taking them on treks around the perimeter of the golf course, losing them in ponds for heart-stopping minutes until they emerged yards away with duck feathers in their jaws. Thinking of Sundays, I can see that we never shed our caravan mentality. Unless it was pouring with rain, we inevitably spilled outside, setting up artists' studios on the front steps, making complex housing estates for soft toys on the lawn. Listen, you can hear the conversations of our neighbours as they tuck in to their dinners.

'Nice bit of lamb this, not New Zealand?'

'No Dear, English. Hurry up with the mint sauce.'

'Oh God, there goes one of them now, just whizzed past the window.'

'Where? Which one?'

'The Darkie with the sad eyes. Must have been on wheels, he'd got up quite a speed.'

'As long as he doesn't hit the car.'

'If only they'd confine themselves to indoors instead of spreading all over the place, like fungus.'

'Fungi, Dear, in the plural.'

'Appropriate simile though. Many hued parasites, sometimes attractive, as in the case of the girl with long black hair, but often deadly poisonous or at least having the ability to give one a severe pain in the belly. Unearthly too, not quite of this world. I'm certain they were spored not spawned.'

'Very clever. If only, as you say, they'd stay indoors. Still, there are so many of them, it'd take a mansion to hold them.'

'Hmm. Or an asylum.'

Ha, ha, ha.

As I said, the Day of Deep Sadness was a Sunday, and it was a scorcher. The sun was relentless and since we didn't possess a hose, the only way for us to cool down was by

wading in one of the golf-course ponds. We had been playing
Indians. Not one of us wanted to be a Cowboy. Why be a
boring Baddie in denim when you could be a glorious
Goodie with a screaming redskin and a headdress of magpie
feathers? Samik looked the most impressive, he had the right
shaped face with skin that cried out to be painted for war.
Around his head he'd strapped one of the dogs' collars,
having first stuffed the holes with quills that pointed skywards and left white tips hanging over his brow. Zulema had
lovingly adorned his cheeks with Mum's brightest, reddest
lipstick and her greenest eyeshadow, in Italian flag fashion.
Slung across his naked shoulder was a felt pouch full of
home-made arrows and in his hand he carried a bow
of willow and strong twine. We all made an effort, but only
Samik looked the part. Off we marched, to the Land Of
Many Waters, a colourful tribe in shorts and flip-flops, with
Fabian, who'd 'borrowed' an old fringed leather jacket of
Mum's, whooping ahead, being the chief. Big Chief Big
Mouth we called him behind his back, but he was Chief
Standing Tall when we addressed him. We made a great deal
of noise as we passed the silent houses in our cul-de-sac but
once we reached the rough at the edge of the golf course,
we began to stalk quietly through the undergrowth. Only
Merry found it hard to get the hang of this. Quiet isn't a
word he understands, or a command he obeys. His continued
warlike whooping sent jays and pigeons flapping from the
trees, made the squirrels panic to the point of performing
dangerous leaps and, no doubt, set the rabbits shivering in
their burrows. At the pond we formed a circle, hands held,
feet sunk happily into the cool muddy water, and squelched
our way through a tribal water dance. As we moved we

chanted a mantra Chief Standing Tall had taught us, a rhythmic little number which I thought sounded more African than American but which, I later discovered, was European in origin. We sang, paused and paced, sang, paused and paced again, in time to the chant. It seemed to us the words concerned the weather and a religious recluse called Jenny Ree:

'Nun (squelch, squelch) rain der rain, (stamp, stamp) nun (slurp, slurp) Jenny Ree getta rain.'

(Fabe was the only one of us kids who listened to the radio, and he'd probably only heard the original song once or twice. Add to that his not speaking a word of French and you might forgive him. Years later I heard 'Non, Je ne regrette rien' being rasped out by Edith Piaff . . . you can imagine how I smiled.)

Once we warriors had cooled down and had a battle or two, we crept back to Fisher's Close. That is, six of us crept but Merry ran on ahead, shouting Whoa, Whoa, Whoa until it seemed his lungs must burst. Ahead of us there was a great clatter, as of metal being thrown against tarmac and a loud cry, as of small boy in pain. Merry had caught his foot in a car-washer's hose, collided with a tin bucket full of soapy water and smashed head first into the curb. By the time we got to him he was a soaking, bloody mess, so much blood and water that it was hard to see where his injury was. Every bit of him that we touched, as we pulled him to his feet, seemed to be either red or pink. People were coming out of their houses, their Sunday peace destroyed yet again by The Cornflake House kids. Everybody was talking at once, some speaking directly to Mum, who had appeared but seemed unable to make another move, some muttering to themselves. I remember only wanting to get away, to drag my bleeding brother home so as to comfort him, heal him and remonstrate with him. If Merry's injury had been less dramatic I might have managed but the blood, diluted with half a bucket of car shampoo, kept on pouring.

'Let my dad have him,' a voice said, 'he's done First Aid, let him do it.' The voice belonged to one Philip Bamford, a boy of ten who hadn't previously thought us worthy of his attention, except to sneer at in passing. His dad, who was now examining Merry gently, was a smallish round man with fat but competent fingers and a bright ginger moustache. He lifted Merry's head, an action that covered his competent fingers with blood. I saw Mr Bamford blanch, for all his having First Aid. A second later I caught the merest glimpse of Merry's chin and no doubt I also did an impression of a sheet. There was something shining in the folds of raw, ripped flesh, something so white it was almost silver. Bone. It was chin bone exposed like a gruesome smile amongst the parted skin.

'Two of you, in the back of the car with him,' Mr Bamford barked, 'hold him down, keep his head up. Out of the way the rest of you.' Fabian and I obeyed mutely, sitting one on each side of Merry in the back of the Bamford's elegant Riley while Mum pressed both her hands against the window and mouthed words we hadn't a chance of hearing. We were in deep shock, accidents hardly ever happened to us, not major ones; Mum usually managed to foresee and forestall them. Until we arrived at the doors of Casualty, I didn't even notice that Philip had slipped into the passenger seat and made the journey to hospital with us.

'My dad's brilliant with things like this,' Philip told us as we sat waiting. He proceeded to describe his own accidents, giving details of the methods of healing practised, in each case, by his amazing father. He used words we'd never heard before, turn-nick-hey, ab-race-shun, until First Aid became, in our eyes, a complex, foreign science and Mr Bamford a professor touched with genius. While we waited and marvelled, doctors, nurses and porters passed us by, each making some apt comment about our appearance:

'Never mind, you'll be back in your tepee before nightfall.'

'Is this a private pow-wow, or can anybody join in?'

One doctor walked by clutching the top of his head, a visual gag it took me some time to understand.

'Your jacket's wrong,' Philip told Fabe. 'It's more Buffalo Bill than Indian.'

'I stole it off him, didn't I?' Fabe responded, quick as a flash. 'At the Battle of Wounded Knee.'

'My dad's got a pair of real moccasins,' boasted Philip. We believed him, we'd have believed him if he'd told us Mr Bamford was actually Sitting Bull himself, in disguise.

And so we passed the time until our brother was brought back to us, guided by his ginger saviour, with a bandage the size of a bedspread wrapped around his swollen chin.

'Six stitches,' Mr Bamford announced, as proud as if he'd done the needlework himself. On the way home Mr Bamford let Merry sit in the front of the Riley while Philip squashed in the back with me and Fabian. I think the man had grown rather fond of the odd little boy, but he made a mistake in letting Merry near his dashboard and his gear stick. At one time, as my brother yanked the stick and sent the car crunching from top to bottom gear, I thought we'd all be back in Casualty any second. This was before the days of seat belts and by leaning forward Merry was able to play with the windscreen wipers, honk the horn and pull danger-ously on the handbrake. Mr Bamford sweated profusely and gave Merry ineffectual pats on the knees. As we pulled into Fisher's Close I'm sure I saw him cross himself in gratitude.

The incident, a frightening combination of hurt, shock and discovery, disturbed Merry deeply. Apart from the pain of his injury, the experience gave him his first encounter with a father. When Mr Bamford was leaving us, having turned down Mum's offer to share a pot of tea, Merry clung to his short legs and howled. It took three of us to pull him off and then to stop him from splitting his chin open again by rolling around on the floor. Mr Bamford made a quick getaway.

'I want . . . a . . . dad, get . . . me a dad,' Merry cried, much as if dads were to be found growing on trees or sitting, complete with pipes and slippers, on the counters of Woolworth's. Within minutes we were all at it, blubbing and muttering, swaying with loss. I think Mum must have capitulated, allowing if not actually encouraging us to begin the second chant of the day, because we seemed compelled to cry out, 'I want a dad,' repeatedly, in unison. She herself joined in, not with words, but with a deep, harmonic moan, a base to our descant.

Afterwards, exhausted and with a sore throat, I felt refreshed somehow. The unspeakable had been mentioned, more than mentioned, dragged out of the cupboard, exam-ined and exorcised. There was the relief of discovering that all my siblings felt as I did, that they too missed their unknown fathers, plus the joy of having been able to share this emotion with Mum; and there was a warm, companionable sensation of being one of a tribe who knew, instinctively, how to emote. We were still dressed for war, but we'd performed a ritual that left us peaceful, contented, united.

'Today,' Mum whispered as she tucked me up in bed, 'was The Day of Deep Sadness, but it was worth it, missing your dads will never be as lonely or as painful again.' Because I liked the day's name, I nodded, although all sadness had been banished as far as I could see.

When I came back from my reverie, Merry was still looking at me as if I might provide answers to all life's problems. Then he must have noticed my bruises. He blew his cheeks out, hamster style, trying to look as ghastly as I did, and I laughed. I'd forgotten how Merry, who has strong men weeping with exhaustion, can make me smile and laugh in dire situations. He took my face in his hands, hurting my sore jaw, and came very close. We were eyeball to eyeball, a favourite position of Merry's. Then I felt myself being turned, like a screw inside a rawlplug. Jim was fast, but not quite quick enough. My neck clicked, a fierce reminder of recent tortures, while Jim's hands joined Merry's and pulled in the opposite direction.

'Sorry,' Jim said, 'I thought he was giving you a cuddle.'

'Probably was, to start with,' my voice sounded as if it was coming through a funnel.

Merry, having been prised from me, was spinning by himself. He can do this for hours, without getting dizzy. Some party piece. Trouble is he toots as he spins, and the warder didn't take kindly to that. Jim shrugged apologetically as they were escorted out. It was several minutes before Merry's demented steam-train noises died away.

At least Merry has a home, with an assortment of friends and carers. I felt more sorry for myself than for him.

He must sound like a walking disaster, my big little brother. You should know Merry as he was before meeting him as he is. Not that there's a great difference between the boy and the man. Merry has stayed childlike, he's grown, but not grown up. He was a smashing kid, infuriating, mind-bogglingly tiring but funny as any circus clown. His pratfalls never failed to have us in stitches. Of course Mum knew when she was carrying him how he would be. The name was no coincidence. His good humour is his saving grace. Merry often harms people, holds them too tight, twists them, treads on them, but never with malicious intent. The problem now is that he's so big. Features which were endearing when he was a little boy, his large, staring eyes, his squashed nose, have spread to grotesque proportions. Hours of exercise, spinning, jumping, running riot, have given him muscles weaklings would kill for. I couldn't help noticing that Jim, who has been caring for Merry for about a year, was looking pretty fit too. The purple ship on his left bicep was riding the crest of an impressive wave.

When I was little and couldn't sleep, I used to imagine how it felt to be Merry. I'd open my eyes so wide they would ache, then I'd stare at something with manic intensity. Fisher's Close was lit by dainty mock-Victorian street lights. A lemon glow filled the bedrooms of The Cornflake House and through this I'd glare at the end of my bed or the wardrobe mirror. I never actually jumped about but I'd bounce on my bottom and turn my head from side to side until I was dizzy. Being Merry for two or three minutes sent me practically into a coma. How he copes with himself day in day out is one of life's unfathomable mysteries. Glands are to blame, I guess, juices flowing through him like electricity. If only they saturated his brain as they do his muscles, he'd be a genius. Imagine that energy and good humour put to use. He might have been capable of anything, politics, business, environmental miracles. I mean if Bing, for example, had Merry's glands, road planners would throw up their hands in defeat. I think this combination has occurred to my son, I've seen him gazing wistfully at his hyperactive uncle.

Complaints from the inhabitants of Fisher's Close centred on Merry. He was the one they remembered, the body they knew best amongst the muddle of Cornflake House children. Mostly they were right, Merry did cause damage. He had no idea of property, or possession. Fences, which sprang up between gardens not long after we moved in, were climbing frames to him. Mr Turner, who had retired to Fisher's Close after long years spent hounding those who didn't pay their taxes, was often to be seen moving at a good speed, considering his advanced years, in pursuit of Merry. Behind Mr Turner lay a flower bed in tatters, in front he brandished his garden fork. It was all a game to Merry, sometimes he turned tail and did the chasing so as to be 'it' for a change.

To be honest, the rest of us often hid our misdoings behind our non-stop brother. He had no problem with taking the blame. He had no problems, full stop. Life for Merry was one long round of activity. Moving, doing, was all. Words meant very little to him. On his first day at school, before it entered my mother's head that this child needed special care, he had to be caught like a wild animal. If the staff had been allowed to use tranquillizer guns, I'm sure they'd have aimed these, without a qualm, at Merry's back-side. He liked school, there was so much to do there. He treated the place like one great leisure centre, splashing through the goldfish pond, skimming up the poles that sup-ported the entrance canopy and swinging doors backwards and forwards with his feet.

Perdita had the task of taking Merry and settling him in. She was starting her final year at primary school, nearly eleven and already bitterly ashamed of her siblings. She arrived home that afternoon in tears, with Merry tied to her by a length of stout rope.

'He might skip,' Perdita had told the teacher whose job it was to get Merry into a classroom.

'Skip?'

'To class. He might think it's a game.'

It worked. Teacher, mortified sister and problem new boy skipped down the corridors to the intake class. Perdita scurried off, leaving Merry to his fate. The real difficulties were about to begin. Merry simply couldn't sit still. For a while he bounced on the spot, or jumped from side to side which was distracting for the others but not too terrible. It was when he struggled up on to his desk that the teacher knew things weren't going to improve. Perdita was called. She arrived to find her brother playing hopscotch from desk to desk while several tiny, bawling children nursed their crushed fingers. They wouldn't tie a child to a chair today, would they? Even in the most impossible circumstances they'd find another solution. But on Merry's first, and last, day at an ordinary school, it seemed the safest, sanest answer. When school was over, the rope was transferred from chair to sister and Merry led Perdita home at breakneck speed.

Perhaps you're thinking that my mother was mad or cruel to send Merry there at all. Remember, she saw only the positive side of her children. To her Merry was a happy, non-aggressive little boy. He wouldn't fight or bully any of his school friends. He'd take part in anything physical with unbounded enthusiasm and he could be relied on to eat every scrap of those soggy school dinners. When Perdita wailed out her story, Mum was genuinely amazed that the day had been a disaster. Long before Perdita got to the part about Merry having been tied to a chair, my mother was blaming the school.

'I'm so disappointed,' she told us, 'I thought they'd be able to cope. It's their job. Besides, they manage with Django.'

At this Perdita let out a snort of disgust and announced that she refused to go to any school that might have to 'manage' both Merry and Django.

'I've suffered enough,' she said through tears of self-pity. 'If you knew what they say about him,' and a trembling finger pointed at Django, 'you'd never dare show your face outside this house.'

Maybe she was right. Mum was rather cushioned by domesticity. Washing for eight, cooking vast meals, cleaning out hutches and birdcages, kept her fairly housebound. Besides, she had the ability to turn a deaf ear, perhaps to actually block out sounds. Snide comments, made whenever we passed through our respectable neighbourhood, bounced from Mum's radar system. She wasn't a vindictive person anyway, not keen on retribution considering how easy it would have been for her. I only recall her once using her power to tick somebody off. She was mean to the Morrisons.

The Morrisons, who lived in the end house, where Fisher's Close meets the outside world, were especially vicious to us. In every other respect the Morrisons were good people, they gave generously to charities, went to church, belonged to the RSPCA. They have been removed now, like Taff, to Homes, their mock-Tudor house taken over and converted into an imitation hacienda by an ambitious builder – from the sublime to the ridiculous – but if I found them and confronted them with their cruelty I imagine they'd be horrified. I put their treatment of us down to a kind of blind spot. They used to hiss at us, snakes in the manicured grass behind their precious privet. They called us 'trampsss' or 'tinkersss', when there was no need. Because they lived a fair distance from us, we gave them little grief. Even Merry was usually caught and dragged away before he reached their gate. Yet they behaved as if our very existence had ruined theirs. I suppose we did lower house prices in Fisher's Close, rather considerably. Anyway, one day, as I hobbled by with Mum on our way to the bus stop, they hissed the word 'Ssslut' at me. I was wearing the white plastic boots and a miniskirt and I crumpled at their taunt. The air lightened, I sensed a breath of something special. My mother waved her arms, not against anything, it was a beckoning motion. Then there were little cries as the dreaded couple began to fight off a swarm of midges who were intent on trying to fly down the throats of the hissing Morrissssonssss.

I tried this trick myself once, on a man who was shuffling his behind closer and closer to mine in a railway waiting room. I closed my eyes, waved my arms and thought 'swarm', picturing wasps by the hundreds. A single gnat materialized before my face.

'Not me, you fool, him,' I said crossly. Then I saw the funny side and laughed out loud. The gnat stayed with me, but the man shot away. When you need to get rid of two-legged pests, talking to yourself works just like magic.

Thinking of two-legged pests, what have I said about Django? I forget. Have you some idea about him? Strange is not the word to describe him, singular comes closer but it hardly does him justice. When Mum was forced to admit Merry needed special care and education, the school found us a social worker, a wholesome young woman called Janet who appeared, to me at any rate, to have stepped straight out of an Enid Blyton book. Janet had a ruddy glow, surely the result of eating simply stacks of thickly cut brown bread and wedges of cheese? Her legs were straight and stocking-less, their tan accentuated by white ankle socks curled around brown sandals. She tended to go for tweeds, not the heavy variety, but light checks or flecks. Her only frivolity was a chiffon scarf she wore wrapped tightly round her neck.

'Do you wear that to hide your wrinkles?' Django asked.

'No, to hide my blushes, which begin there and work their way upwards,' Janet answered, blushing on cue. From that moment Mum loved Janet.

'Can you do something about him while you're at it?' Mum wondered, indicating Django who had stopped staring at Janet, having got a satisfactory answer, and was re-examining the parts of an Electrolux 'Portable Cleaning Unit' he had found at a jumble sale. I remember the name because every time one of us tripped over the damn thing, we'd shout, 'Django, put that bloody Hoover away.'

And he'd correct us, 'It's not a Hoover, it's an Electrolux Portable Cleaning Unit.' He had the original box to prove his point, although this had been left in the sunny window of a shed and now read 'rolu able ning nit', a description the rest of us found appropriate.

'Obsessive?' Janet guessed. She attempted to whisper but her voice wasn't designed for quiet. Mum nodded. Janet promised to do her best and before long Merry and Django were sharing outings to a child psychiatrist in London. (A while back, Zulema and I confessed to each other that for a short time after hearing of the child psychiatrist, we both pictured an under-age doctor struggling with our brothers.)

Because the first trip was so fraught – Merry wanted to get into the luggage rack on the train and Django refused to travel without half a Hoover under his arm – Mum decided to take Fabian, then a surly boy of thirteen, to help and support her through the second visit. The child psychiatrist was, to Mum's consternation, much more interested in Fabian than in the two younger boys. He positively shone with enthusiasm the moment he saw Fabe. Apparently the shrink was midway through a paper on teenagers of mixed racial origins. What especially delighted him was Fabe's refusal to cooperate:

'You feel an outcast?' the man guessed hopefully as Fabian pouted at him. 'You suffer from a feeling that you don't belong?'

'No,' Mum chipped in, 'he's sulking because Merry,' she had the child in question clamped between her legs, 'trod on his guitar and we can't afford to mend it. Merry does that, breaks things, he's always on the go.' What was the use? She'd been through this before, trying to describe the indescribable, and it seemed to be getting her nowhere.

The last thing she needed was for someone to decide that Fabian was a problem too.

For the third visit she chose me as travelling companion and helper.

'He won't be nearly so interested in you,' she promised. I was sitting on Merry in a crowded train compartment at the time. It was the only way to control him. Nothing daunted, he jogged his captured body to the rhythm of the train. Having suffered the motion in stereo, I was quite queasy by the time we reached Waterloo. I was fourteen, an age at which I found my family mortifying under any circumstances, and the looks on the faces of our fellow travellers are clearly imprinted on my memory. Not only were they compelled to watch a fat, tangle-haired girl sit on a weird little boy while glaring at another freakish child who appeared to have a vacuum cleaner welded to his armpit, but the conversation they overheard must have sounded obscene.

'It's only boys like Fabian that get him going,' Mum continued, 'that's why I've left him with the animals this time.'

Several passengers dropped their newspapers in dismay.

'Course, by rights,' she carried on, oblivious, 'he should have noticed Django's colour, but he's too young. Teenagers, he said, and you should have seen him, Eve, he was practically dribbling with excitement over your dark-skinned brother.'

Brothers, I thought, from rising rock stars to domestic appliance fanatics, who needs them? Only little Samik, who was tearful and insecure but otherwise fairly 'normal', was worth bothering with.

That was my fourteen-year-old attitude. I love my

brothers, I always did, just had a patch of embarrassment in my teens. You know about Fabian, I suppose? He's famous, or he was. Recently he's gone beyond famous to that tranquil place rock stars seem to seek after years of blasting music and deafening applause. He had a good time, sex, drugs – I remember the glazed eyes only too well – and rock and roll. Then suddenly it ended. One final shattering chord and he was done.

'I'm going acoustic,' he told me and Mum the last time he came to The Cornflake House, 'going to play in small cafés, on beaches, round camp fires, that sort of thing. Quiet, I'm into that. Soft,' and he kissed Mum's cheek goodbye. Whether he meant to, hoped to see her again I couldn't say. He'll stay away, even when my trial comes up, I'm pretty sure of that. Shan't see those cinnamon eyes, those long, talented fingers again. Unless you and I take a trip to a particularly remote Greek island and wander down, on a balmy evening, for a drink at the local bar.

Meanwhile, back at the psychiatrist's, Merry was being classified as hyperactive and educationally subnormal, while Django continued to baffle the disappointed doctor.

'No Fabian today?' he asked unnecessarily, and Mum gave me an I-told-you-so smile.

Merry's labels made it possible for him to get special care and that freed the rest of us to an extent. He lived at home until he was sixteen, mind you. Then his libido went into overdrive and nothing was safe. I wasn't there when they drove Merry away. It happened when Bing was tiny and I was trying to bring up a baby and study Literature in a damp North London flat. I heard the stories of Merry's sexual exploits later and I had to laugh, although it wasn't funny.

Not for Mum anyway. She'd always thought of Merry as her worst failure. Oh, she could subdue him for minutes, even hours at a time, and sometimes she channelled his energy from destructive to constructive, but she never managed to conjure real, long-term peace for him.

I went home for a weekend not long after Merry left and was struck by the emptiness of the living room. It seemed almost large with only Mum, Bing and me occupying it.

Samik hadn't fled the nest, of course, but he'd discovered rivers, canals and boats as ardently as Merry had discovered sex and was down in Guildford trying to get a holiday job on some narrow boat.

'Merry didn't seem to mind,' Mum told me, 'went off happy as a lark. They've got a trampoline and an electric organ. I went to see the place, of course. It's very bright, sliding glass doors everywhere. I told them to watch him with those and they said it was all right, the glass was toughened.' For the first time, I noticed how my mother had aged. There was grey in her ebony hair and although I saw no wrinkles, her skin lacked something, colour, elasticity. I couldn't bear it, this indication that she was mortal and fading.

'I'd like to come home.'

'Why don't you come back home?'

We spoke simultaneously. We often did.

Before he left The Cornflake House, Merry went to special school, but Django plodded on at the local primary and later at the comprehensive. He never was given labels. Whether that lack was a blessing or a curse I've no idea. For a while the psychiatrist thought he was autistic, a diagnosis based on Django's obsessive behaviour.

'His need to repeat patterns, his overwhelming interest, to the exclusion of all else, in one topic, in Django's case the workings of vacuum cleaners, these are our indications,' the shrink told Mum. She wasn't convinced; and her instinct was right. Several weeks later, after Django had told the psychiatrist many truths about himself, the man changed his mind. He said it was another syndrome altogether, this time citing Django's want of social grace as the basis for his findings:

'He has no concept of correct social behaviour, I have advised him many times that telling me I have, for example, hairs in my ears, is not a nice, friendly thing to do. But your Django is unable to see the difference between the things we should and should not say.'

'He tells the truth,' Mum said, no doubt giving the doctor cause to wonder if Django's problems were inherited.

'Absolutely, but he cannot distinguish between the truths most of us keep to ourselves and those we may speak out loud.'

Django lives in Chatham now, he chose it because of the docks. He has a flat within walking distance of the ships that interest him so. At school he only ever developed one talent, apart from the ability to mend the cleaners' equipment for them, and that was in geography. In those days the subject was colourful; pink blotches, yellow continents, blue oceans. Books were illustrated with drawings of tribes out hunting, crossing deserts, paddling canoes down wide green rivers. Django was brilliant at maps, spending hours with his face inches from the paper, perfecting every cove and inlet. Ultimately this passion overtook his love of vacuum cleaners. I've often considered Django's luck. If Mum and I hadn't got the order of those electrical gadgets just right in our competition, we wouldn't have had a house, let alone a Hoover. What would Django have done then? He might have become intensely withdrawn, staring into space, longing for something he couldn't name. Who knows? Fate is often a kind beast.

As I say, maps took over from cleaners, and now he works for a company who publish maps old and new. Having ruined his eyes with the close work, he wears thick glasses which, I discovered when I went to look after him one time when he was ill, he puts on at seven-ten a.m. precisely, after unbuttoning his pyjama top but before taking his arms out of this garment.

It's true that maps won the day from Hoovers, but it was an uphill struggle. I once took Django with me to a party, he was seventeen and I thought it time he met some other teenagers. He wouldn't drink because I'd forgotten to take his special cup, and I knew there was no point in offering him a snack. He only ever ate his own 'meal', a red and green affair of peas, placed in a mound, centre plate, two whole lettuce leaves curling upwards, opposite each other, and one tomato sliced in half and laid, wounded side down, on the lettuce. But the party appeared to be going well, Django was talking to another boy, advising this lad on ways of banishing spots, when I went to dance with my boyfriend.

Then I lost him. He'd vanished. I thought he'd walked home. I wasn't that worried, he was seventeen and he knew where he lived. Several hours later there was a cry from a girl who'd gone to fetch her coat from the understairs cupboard. There was Django, bent over the party-giver's rather ancient vacuum, a tubular object that he'd taken to bits, sitting with a torch in his hands. He held his light before his face as people gathered to stare at him. The ghost of Hoovers past.

Can't see many signs of innate, genetic behaviour patterns in Django's case, can you? It's unlikely that his Gypsy dad was riveted by the workings of domestic appliances. No self-respecting Romany would admit to that hobby when they should be out catching rabbits and breaking horses:

'Sorry, Jo, can't come down the paddock with you until I've oiled me Hoover.'

Hardly the picture of life on the road we have been taught to cherish.

When I felt close to Mum and sensed that questions about our fathers, a taboo subject in my family, might not be met with unease, it was usually Django's dad I asked about.

I found it impossible to envisage my own father, and I was scared of doing so. Much as we were filled with fascination and yearning for our dads, we Cornflake House kids lived under their shadows too. Who knows? These almost phantom men might come at any time and reclaim us, whisking us away. These scenes of abduction altered, for me, as I grew. When I was little, in Lincolnshire, my dreams were of a huge, sandy-haired man who wore sandals, so I wouldn't hear his coming I suppose. It was always night and there was a full moon in that dream landscape. He was big but agile, and he carried a sack. As he swung his way to my bedside, leaping over ditches and dikes, he plucked small animals from the ground and crushed their bones with his bare hands. His sack grew heavier as he approached. By the time he arrived, squeezing his frame through the caravan door, the sack was so full it had to be dropped by my bed as he bent to lift me.

'You're mine,' he breathed. I shivered in my nightie, shrank from his beer and tobacco breath, but never offered any resistance as he picked me up on his shoulder. It was only when he opened his sack and I saw the mess of flesh, fur and blood, that I struggled.

'In you go,' he said, not unkindly, it was more of a tease, but as he tipped me, head first down into the death sack I kicked and bit and screamed. I used to wake, or sometimes be woken by Zulema, a second before my head collided with the poor animals.

'Was it your "father dream"?' she'd ask. She had her own recurring nightmare involving her own imagined father. We all did, they were so swathed in mystery, our dads, it was only to be expected. Zulema's dream involved white horses and gentle rides across plains of meadow grasses. At the same point in her journey, just when she felt she was getting to know and love her father, he would suggest a gallop and race on ahead. But her horse would rear up and throw her to the ground. Instead of rescuing her, her father would turn in the distance and gallop back to her, not stopping but letting his beast thunder closer and closer. When Zulema woke with a start I knew she had just leapt to her feet to avoid being trampled to death.

My dad shrank as I grew. The sack became a trunk, then the boot of a car, but there was always a dark place in which he wanted to throw me. Not was, is; I still dream of him. My subconscious has allowed him to age, letting his hair fade from sand to ash, but the expression on his face hasn't altered. He peers at me with greed, 'You're mine,' he says, possessively, and I can only suppose that a part of me likes this idea of being wanted, for whatever reason.

No, I never asked about my own father, fearing the worst, perhaps even fearing the best. What if he's a wonderful man, bright, intelligent, witty? Think of how much I might have missed. Now that I'm motherless, I wish I'd been braver, more inquisitive, and found out who he is while I still had the chance. On the other hand, for all I know, he may have been in contact with Mum from the day I was born. If so the least he could do now is to get in touch, to hear my side of the story. This is one place where his agility would come in handy, the only place I've lived where being rescued, even if rescue meant being shoved in a sack, would be a treat.

The little girl in me says 'what the hell, he wouldn't love me anyway'. Our dads; did they ever have a chance? Or were they discouraged by Mum and her magic? As I said, when I felt able, I did ask the odd question about Django's father; and I got the odd answer.

'He was a rough one all right,' Mum once admitted.

'Was he really a Gypsy?'

'Oohh yes, warts and all.'

'And was he obsessive, like Django?'

'Only about sex,' Mum grinned. 'Sex and sugar. He ate sweeties all the time. Humbugs.'

That was about it. Either she would drift to a world of fantasy, making up stories she thought I'd enjoy, or she'd make my head fizz until I dropped the subject and went to find the aspirin.

Ten minutes to lights out. Can you imagine what it's like to have your life regulated by somebody else? I am tired, but I shan't sleep. There is more I'd like to tell you. But it's lights out and I'm condemned to lie in the dark. Remembering. Alone. Panic struck. I've had a change of heart, Matthew. I do want to see you, I need to talk to a friend. I need to repeat, out loud, the accusations hurled by the women who attacked me in the toilet. They called me Mother Fucker, and it shocked me, but it's just an expression, an Americanism, isn't it? I could live with that. Then they called me Mother Killer. And that's what Valerie was trying to tell me earlier. Somebody somewhere has got hold of the idea that I *killed* my mother.

'We don't take kindly to Mother Killers here,' they said as they kicked the shit out of me. Numb with shock as I was, I didn't respond. Later I almost laughed. It was ridiculous, the thought of me taking the life of my mum, destroying the thing I lived for. Yet it seems likely that I shall be tried for exactly that.

Nine

I walked with caution, aware of movement over my shoulder, expecting the sudden onslaught of fresh violence but I was still eager, if not exactly light of foot, when heading down the corridor to see you.

Thanks for your discretion, Matthew, and for the good advice; deep breathing, yes, I'll try that, and thinking positively, well, again I'll make the effort. Although it won't be easy, when the only certainty is that the rest of the world is lined up against me. I'd never have thought that the day would come when I was afraid of almost everybody.

Sorrow and nervousness are eating my insides. Causing weight loss; there, a positive thought. I must have mislaid several pounds with all the worry. I used to eat in times of crisis, as if buns and biscuits would cure a broken heart or get me through exams. It was a whale who sat my GCEs for me. Come to think of it, I used to eat in times of calm too. Meals in The Cornflake House were random affairs, it was a case of grab it while it was there or go without. Mum was an unwilling cook, not a regular meal-giver, not one who prepared food when it was needed. She cooked when she saw us pigging too many snacks. She could mix a cake as light as air or blend herbs and spices to make mouth-watering stews when the mood took her, but the mood didn't take her nearly often enough. We kids developed arm actions to accompany meals and some of these, embarrassingly enough, linger on. If you and I ever settle down to enjoy a quiet dinner in a smart restaurant, please feel free to place your hand on mine when I seem to be diving across the table to grasp the last remaining bread roll. No, I'll be fine really, either my glands have altered, or prison food has worked a transformation on my psyche. Somehow I'm not tempted to eat myself stupid anymore. An entrepreneur could make a fortune by prescribing instant mashed potato and lumpy gravy as a cure for obesity.

Since I'm hated for having cut myself off from company, perhaps I should write to other people, not confine my letter writing to you. I have been getting post, as it happens. I suspect Valerie of circulating my address, possibly even of writing to my family for character references, then adding a postscript to say she thinks I might appreciate letters or cards. I had a postcard from Fabian. Sea, sand, outrageously blue sky, made me long for freedom. I miss the weather. Of course I go outside but I'm unaware of the skies, in general. I'm excused exercise, my back hasn't recovered well, sudden movements bring spasms of pain to my spine. Flitting from block to block is about my limit now so I'm not out there long enough to notice what kind of day it is. And I haven't seen a night sky for months. No doubt the stars shine on, the moon glides through her phases, but all unseen by me. Whereas Fabian probably sleeps under a clear star-studded sky most nights. He didn't say much, always a master of the understatement, Fabe, but it's good to know he cares and that he lays no blame at my feet.

Then there was a letter from Perdita, written on a computer. It was her first communication with me since Mum died, so of course there was a lot about how sad she is, sincerely heart-rending stuff which made me sorry not to have seen her in person. On the other hand, she's also furious with me, not, as far as I can make out, for committing a crime, but for having been sent to a dump like this, thus bringing shame upon her head. I shan't reply to that one and I won't write back to Fabian because I can think of nothing suitable to say until I have definite news about my fate. The third piece of post is unopened. I know who it's from, the post mark and the smell of violets do rather give the game away. Taff. What's that old bat got to say to me? Must be something she thinks is important, I've never known her write to anyone before. I wasn't aware that she *could* write. Maybe she dictated it to some adoring old man. I can't bring myself to open the envelope. I'm afraid of all the memories and accusations buried in there, gasping for an airing.

Why should I suffer from guilt? Have you met this consequence before? Where the imprisoned grow accustomed to believing they're in the wrong? Between you, me and whoever has the job of reading these letters, I might be going a little mad. Stress, I suppose. My case is due in court any day. Scared? Yes, shitless.

I wonder who'll write to me next. Maybe I'll receive one of those hippy prayers from Zulema. She lives in a commune, with a group of weirdos who have dedicated their lives to the moon and the sun. It seems they are fine and dandy as long as there's light in the sky. On moonless winter nights, after sunless days, depression rules, suicides are almost commonplace. It's not a strict sect, they're allowed out, to shop, to pay visits, but mostly they choose not to leave their circle of huts, situated just off a motorway in Gloucestershire. Zulema is especially reluctant to make journeys. She joined them because she was attacked by two men one night; one moonless night, of course. To those of us who saw Zulema when the thugs had finished with her, and shared in her horror, the move to the sect made perfect sense. Where else might she have gone? She was too shaken, rendered too insecure, to sit in The Cornflake House garden unless there was another member of the family with her. So yes, we were full of understanding when she packed a bag and left for her hut. Not that understanding helped to ease the pain of losing her.

She's a dark, mysterious creature, her movements always graceful, her voice low and calming. Zulema has skin the colour of milky coffee and hair that hangs down to her waist. Once she stopped biting her nails, there was nothing jagged about her. She flows and floats through life.

Apart from Mum, I miss Zulema the most. I was closer to her than any of the others. As children we stood up for each other, invented games together, shared our toys. Like me, she inherited the ability to see what was coming, to predict and occasionally to change events. But she was nervous of using her magic; when she did put it to use it was only ever to improve a person's lot. No amount of coaxing could persuade her to do wrong. For example, she never joined in our taunting of Taff.

I once wasted a whole summer's afternoon begging

Zulema to help me create a tidal wave in a pond. It was only a small pond, on the edge of the golf course opposite Fisher's Close, so I wasn't prompting a major environmental disaster. Two particularly obnoxious boys were rowing around this little haven, terrorizing shoals of fish and families of ducks. We could have upset their boat and dumped them head first in the water if we'd put both our minds to it. While I tried and failed to stir the waters by myself, Zulema stood at the pond's edge, her attention divided equally between willing me to stop devising horrid punishments for the boys and willing the lads to turn from their evil ways and become keen naturalists. All this wishing she managed without speaking a word, the only sign of life was her eyes moving sadly from one miscreant to the other.

She always was a little strange. The interest in the moon didn't start with the sect. When she read about them in one of Mum's occultish magazines, Zulema grew excited and said that she'd found her soulmates. Even as a tiny child Zulema's moods shifted with the moon's phases, and naturally as she grew up her menstrual cycle waxed and waned with the moon. I've often wondered if my sister is the only one who is truly in tune, or if the rest of the hut-dwellers are also sincerely motivated by that silver satellite. I'll tell you a secret. When the moon was full Zulema used to sleep on the landing. It was the only place in The Cornflake House where the glow could bathe her. There are people who can't sit out of the sun, if the sun shines, who get tetchy in the shade or indoors on bright days, Zulema is like that about moonshine. When she left, she gave me one of her pendants, a crescent opal, to remember her by. I never wore it, instead Mum and I hung it in the kitchen window where it winked at us and gleamed whitely. I can see it now, not hanging, spinning on its thread, but severed as it was on the night my mother died.

It was a great sacrifice I made, on my mother's behalf. I deserve praise, for being strong willed and obedient, rather than punishment.

I say that Zulema would only use her magic to improve a situation, but I suppose Mum was equally restrained. There was one time, in a queue for fruit and veg, when a fellow shopper pushed in front of me and Mum, then trod on Mum's foot. I knew by the scowl on my mother's brow that this shopper was about to suffer. When the woman's bag was full, it burst open, spilling greens and apples on the shop floor. As she bent, cursing, to pick these up, the food came alive in her hands. Cabbages and fruit which had been green and healthy seconds before were suddenly covered in maggots and flies. The insects clambered over the woman's hands and up her arms as if bug heaven lay above, in her armpits.

Retribution can be sweet. I've been tempted to name the women who attacked me, or the ring-leader at least. I know her; she's the one who tried to 'tax' me by taking my Saturday biscuits. I'm too afraid of repercussions to give in to the temptation, a fear she banks on when putting in the boot, no doubt. Nobody names names here. I must have made a bitter enemy when I clung to my little packet of Rich Teas. Funny to think of her stewing in her cell, plotting how to get back at me. How pleased she must have been when she heard about the new charge, it made it easy for her to drum up support you see. Almost everybody hates a 'mother killer'. It's a pity my magic has ceased to work. Before it left me so abruptly, I could have made her itch all over or given her a nasty dose of the runs. She ought to suffer somehow, though, don't you think, for having irrevocably damaged my confidence? It's impossible for me to conceive of standing in a court, never mind speaking up for myself. Come to that, I'm not sure if I can speak, my mouth's in such a state. Did I talk to you? I don't recall uttering a single word since I was beaten. Oh yes, I spoke to Merry; it must have been the first time we actually sounded as if we were related. I shall try another word now; two syllables, no prizes for guessing what they are.

Well, a sound of sorts, a poor thing. The 'M' is difficult, let's hope I'm not obliged to say 'Me Lord' frequently. Court; the idea fills me with dread, sending my mind on a crash course of history, cases and outcomes through the ages. On the toilet floor I discovered that some think beheading is too soft a punishment for the likes of me. Valerie smiles at our meetings but I see she has little faith in my case. As this rolling stone speeds downhill, I'm beginning to think my mother asked too much of me, not looking, for once, into the future at all. I wrote down the events of the last days of Mum's life. It's the truth, in black biro on white paper, but who knows if anyone will believe it? I would show it to you but I've already given it to Valerie. She wasn't overjoyed, funnily enough. Is she reticent because I've written a confession, more or less, or because she hopes to plead temporary insanity on my behalf? If it's the old mad-with-anxiety plea, I can see her point. My statement doesn't give the impression of a woman who is out of her mind. Words do little to express my feelings, in this case, so I aimed for being matter of fact; and that's what Valerie got, a list of facts.

This is a terrible time for me to be falling, or to have fallen, in love. Life as I knew it ended so violently and since that night my emotions have been raging around. It's exhausting. If, oh let's be hopeful and say when, I get out of here, I shall go to Fabian's island and sleep for three days and three nights. That is if I go alone. Should you decide to come with me, I promise to make every effort to stay awake.

I could do with a holiday. They're oddities, aren't they? We take them to relax but they say a trip abroad can cause as much stress as a divorce or house move. Not that I'd know; I never married, never moved home and only had one 'proper' holiday in my life. During that, the only expedition we made when I was a child, Fabian remarked, ironically enough, 'Prison would be a holiday compared to this.'

Is my life going in circles, or have I developed a selective memory? Needless to say, my childhood holiday was won for me by my mother. Not as exciting as it sounds, please expel all images of coconut trees and white, unruffled sand. I had ideas along the same lines at the time and was bitterly disappointed. Believe it or not, I used to be tormented by greed as a child. You see, we could have had anything, because when your mother has powers, anything is possible. But Mum set herself strict limits. She kept her gains within these confines, trying to instil in us an understanding of want. It wasn't easy, making do with second best when you knew full well that a bit more effort could have won first prize.

Once, I was about nine I think and at the local village fête, I saw a flicker of doubt cross my mum's face, witnessing the moment of decision. She was buying tickets for a raffle. The prizes included a walking, talking doll. It was every little girl's dream, blonde with a rosebud mouth, wearing a pink gingham frock and miniature white ankle socks. Standing at Mum's side, I grinned, imagining myself taking this cute creature for a stroll around Fisher's Close, showing the doll off to Fiona Powell. Fiona, who lived in a pretend Elizabethan monstrosity about three doors from us, was a pretty, spoilt blonde whose mother would have moved mountains to buy her anything she wanted; but the doll wasn't for sale. The raffle provided a rare chance for me to go one better than this brat. 'Mumma,' the doll would have said as we passed Fiona's black and white residence. Dolls had never really interested me, if I wanted to dress and undress small beings, there was always a younger brother or sister needing attention; but this raffle doll wasn't a replica of real life, she came from an alien, exciting world where all eyes were sapphire blue and knickers never got soiled. Besides, I wanted that prize because I knew Fiona had her beady eye on it.

As I said, I saw Mum falter for a second while she chose her tickets. I knew something was up and was disappointed but not surprised when we won, not the doll but a bottle of home-made elderberry wine, undrinkable stuff unless your name is Taff and you visit friends at Christmas and consume everything in sight. The doll went to an old man in a Panama hat. He looked baffled rather than pleased by his win. I remember following him around the fête for the greater part of the afternoon. The soles of the doll's pale pink plastic shoes stuck out under his arm, enticing as ice-cream. He only put the doll down once, while he bought himself a cup of tea, and as I sneakily touched her nylon hair with my fingertips, I marvelled on life's injustices.

The holiday was similar. Mum won it for me because I needed a break from home, but she couldn't bring herself to spoil me even then, so she won a second-rate stay in a cheap part of Spain. I was recovering from glandular fever and a broken heart at the time. Either of these infirmities can lay a teenage girl low for weeks. Put the two together and your patient may seem to be terminally ill.

In my case the glandular fever came first, leading, through my absence from the social whirl of early evening parties and Youth Club, to loss of love and the breaking of my frustrated heart.

The name of the love in question was Marcus Zimmer. An exotic boy, self-assured, easy on the eye. Smooth is the word for him, a smooth operator with shining, unruffled hair and the olive skin of a Greek god. To this day I've never seen eyelashes to match his, or a pair of legs so beautiful.

'Oh dear,' Mum said, putting her arm around my shoulders on the Saturday Marcus and his family moved into the house opposite ours. I was ten at the time and he was twelve. As those long, tanned legs darted in and out of his front door, exploring his new space, I was no less thrilled than if I'd suddenly sighted deer running through Fisher's Close.

It was spring and we'd just inherited a horse from an unknown benefactor. Mum had whispered to me that she believed it had been left in our garden by Django's father, the Gypsy. As she rarely mentioned fathers, I'd felt a current of excitement and envy when told this. I couldn't stretch my imagination far enough to guess what kind of present my own dad might have brought for me, but I longed for something as big and mysterious as the horse to arrive from him. Ironically, of all us children, Django was the least interested in the horse; he might have liked it, had it run on electricity, but flesh and blood meant nothing to him. The poor horse was groomed until he was sore that day. I stood brushing his coat, unmatting his mane, untangling his tail, my eyes on the house opposite, my mind intent on the affect I was having on that tantalizing new boy. I was hot and uncomfortable, having changed, inappropriately for playing at being a groom, from my habitual shorts and tee-shirt into a long sleeved blouse and an embroidered skirt. The skirt was the only one, apart from my grey school uniform, that I possessed. Not only was I baking, I grew cross too, with the horse who, being tempted by the long grass of our front garden, refused to keep his head up. Then I was angry with Merry who insisted on using my bent back as a springboard from which to mount the horse. The animal itself was nothing more or less than a slide to Merry. Then, to top it all, Django appeared:

'Are you going country dancing?' he asked me.

I shook my head, trying to push him away with my free hand.

'Only you said last week,' Django spoke loudly and much too clearly, 'that you hated that silly skirt because it stuck out like a lampshade, and Mum told you that everyone has to wear stuff they hate for country dancing, and you said all right but not at any other time and now you've got it on and you're not even going . . .'

'Here,' I pulled a bribe from my pocket and handed it to him, 'take this and go away.' He did. I always kept some parts of a vacuum cleaner handy, they were essential tools for those who wanted a quiet life.

What can Marcus have thought of us? A family of tramps with a horse and an old cream caravan in our front garden. We also kept chickens, just a small clutch. They were pets really, we ate their eggs but not their flesh. Each had a name and a personal space in the caravan, now doubling up as a hen-house. Taff was staying with us when one snowy white hen, glorying in the name of Ariadne, passed away. There was much wailing and gnashing of teeth, especially from Zulema who claimed, posthumously, that Ariadne had been her own darling chick. So grief-sticken was my beautiful but over-emotional sister that she fetched from our bedroom a large wooden treasure chest, from which she'd emptied her many bracelets and hairbands. With due ceremony the limp corpse was placed in this container and carried, followed by a procession of sombre-faced children, through the kitchen where Taff was chopping vegetables and wondering what else to give us for dinner.

'What you got there?' Taff asked.

'Ariadne,' I whispered, Zulema having been rendered speechless by her grief.

'Arry had what?'

'One of the chickens, she's dead.' I didn't expect Taff to share our sorrow, but I wasn't prepared for her flippancy either.

'Problem solved,' she beamed, 'guess what we'll have for dinner?'

Fourteen eyes stared at her in horror.

'Chicken in the casket.'

She was humming as she turned back to her parsnips and

swedes. We reckoned, as we dug a hole in the grass, that Taff had been only joking but Ariadne was still laid to rest with undignified haste.

Later, because we hadn't pressed the turf down over the grave, one of the dogs dug her up and, having opened the chest with his nose, dragged the dead bird around until the garden looked like the floor of a chicken plucking factory. When she recovered, Zulema, being a rare combination of emotional and practical, rescued her treasure chest, cleaned it and eventually filled it once more with beads and baubles which were easier on the eye and a lot less smelly than a dead chicken.

Ariadne's sister, or auntie, or grandmother, Henrietta (Fabian's choice of name), was pecking about on the doorstep while I groomed the horse and gazed across the road. For the first time I was touched with shame. Those trim houses, our neighbour's gardens with water fountains and up-and-over garage doors, they didn't look so bad after all. Why hadn't we got a car, a red one to shine in our drive? I stood dejected, avoiding the horse's droppings, and surveyed The Cornflake House. Everything was chipped, overgrown, tatty. When was Mum going to get the window mended? That cardboard blocking the hole looked ghastly, especially as it was the side of a box which had once carried toilet rolls and said so in glaring red lettering.

Amazingly, my luck was in. Marcus wasn't necessarily impressed by me, but he thought the horse was wonderful. I gasped as I saw those legs crossing the tarmac to our house.

'Do you use him to pull your cart?' he asked, having introduced himself and got a muttered 'Eve' out of me. It took a couple of seconds for light to dawn, then I instantly wished for the return of dimness. He really did think we were tinkers, scrap merchants, rag-and-bone folks. Blushing to my scalp, I looked down at my filthy feet which were only inches from the horse's latest offering. Finally I managed to move my head stiffly from side to side. Marcus was patting the horse, smiling like a toothpaste advertisement. For once I was glad to see Django, who reappeared by my side.

'Your legs are like polished wood,' he told Marcus, a comment so true it made me snort, a sound Marcus misinterpreted as laughter. We made *him* laugh anyway, between us, Django and I.

After that I led Marcus inside to meet the rest of my family, introducing him proudly, as if I'd crafted him myself. Later we named the horse together, first bouncing ideas around each other, then offering the animal the chance to show his approval or otherwise by chanting into his nostrils. He seemed to like Cecil, so Cecil he was. I longed for Monday and a chance to display Marcus at school, but his parents were rich enough to pay for his education and he was whisked away in a smart black Rover while I sat waiting for my bus. It took me four years to win his heart: twelve school terms, much trickery and many temptations to make him mine. For some reason I assumed that he would love me if I was weaker and more sickly than I appeared to be and I was often to be found limping, coughing and generally fading to a mere shadow in his presence. None of this had any affect, of course. It was money that brought him to my side; it finally happened on another spring Saturday.

Saturdays. Do you remember those teenage Saturdays? The agony of being left dateless and at home while the world partied. The ecstasy of having somewhere to go and somebody worth going there with. Throughout the week it loomed, Saturday night, either empty and depressing as death, or too golden, too frenzied for a soul to bear. At fourteen I felt the degradation of being housebound and boyfriendless on Saturdays profoundly. My problem was being a close neighbour of the boy I loved. How could I forget Marcus and flirt contentedly with less exceptional beings when I saw him every day? Six days of the week I was filled with dreams and possibilities but when Saturday came around I was forced to face a cold truth; I was getting nowhere. I never asked my mother to help, not in Marcus's case. It mattered too much, I needed to know that I'd succeeded or failed by myself. It was first love, and it hurt like hell.

Lord knows how I came to be at the bus stop alone, without the usual flock of relatives in tow, on that fateful Saturday morning, but there I sat, dangling my legs, picking at the oak tree's bark. There was a stop but no shelter, so those of us who waited for the cantankerous number sixty-three, the bus to Woking, used the oak as seat and canopy. In its early days this vast tree must have suffered from a trauma because its trunk grew along the ground, not upwards, for the first six feet, then it turned at a relieved right angle and did what trees should do, pointed to the sky. It made a perfect bench, a seat smoothed by the bottoms of many reluctant schoolchildren. Buses were stubborn in those days, in that part of the world. Although the sixty-three had to chug up the hill, passing Fisher's Close at about two miles an hour, it didn't stop by our houses. As they hadn't been built when the route was laid out, they were ignored. The driver would stop on remote corners to let old women off or to drop more privileged children at their doors, but only if these remote corners had been inhabited from the day that buses were invented. Kindly, obstinate and never, ever on time, that was the sixty-three.

For me, bus travel, kissing and Murray Mints are inextricably linked. I used to suck those smooth, oval sweets as I waited in my leafy shelter; and I'm almost certain that there was a slip of one left in my mouth when Marcus finally shuffled along to find my lips with his. If we were playing Botticelli, if Marcus was a sweet, he'd be a Murray Mint, flawless, flavoured to the core. Add to this the way the sixty-three bus was bullet shaped, cream with green trim, and considered itself too good to hurry, and you have an explanation that would have satisfied Freud himself.

I've almost managed to blank from my memory the fact that Marcus, unusually, was broke that morning and needed to borrow the bus fare. I was the only other passenger, so he asked me for a loan, after he had kissed my astonished lips. I would have walked the five miles to town, gladly waving *my* fare goodbye, for that kiss; but I'd begun working, babysitting for local families, and was wealthy enough for two. We rode side by side, both hushed by what had passed between us; I guess, while I was stunned with pleasurable surprise, Marcus was perplexed by his foolhardiness. He'd needed only to ask and I would have handed him my life's savings; but he had kissed me. A kiss was a seal, it meant much, much more than it does now. You didn't press your lips against another's unless you intended to be, if only for a short time, theirs.

And mine he was, as we ambled around Woking that Saturday morning. I meant to buy personal items, sanitary towels for my new status as a woman with periods, Amplex tablets in case . . . but too late for that now. Not having the courage to visit Boots the chemist with Marcus, I spent my money on records – the ones he liked – and refreshments for both of us. The coffee bar and the park were meeting places for young people; my dreams came true as I sat first on painted chairs drinking a steaming, frothy cappuccino, then on damp grass licking an ice lolly, showing Marcus off to girls my age or older. A return journey on the sixty-three took us to his house to listen to the new records. Everything he owned, including his record player, was more modern and expensive than in The Cornflake House. We'd managed to reduce our own prize gadgets to scrap by then.

I'd not been invited inside Marcus's house before; I hadn't expected ever to walk through that front door. As I did, I had my first encounter with good taste. His mother had chosen furniture, wall and floor coverings and each of her ornaments with extreme care. Even the books might have been selected for the beauty of their spines. The rooms had colour themes, blues shading from delphinium to forget-me-not in the dining room, a bright green and white kitchen and grey walls with red paintwork in Marcus's bedroom – in which, I hasten to add, we merely lounged and listened.

Later, being mine, Marcus suggested we go to Youth Club together. Saturday night, a date, and no Amplex tablets; my heart wasn't so much racing as speeding dangerously. I staggered across the road to attempt the impossible conversion of self into superstar. After several hours of bathing, shampooing and worrying, I looked much the same as before, only redder in the face from steam and stress. It's hard to imagine, it wasn't easy to believe at the time, but we, the world's most unlikely couple, had fun together. Carried on a high of disbelief, exhilaration and vodka, stolen from his father's drinks cabinet and slipped into my orange juice by my thoughtful date, I sailed through the evening, not the most beautiful girl in the church hall but by far the most amusing. When Marcus kissed me goodnight on The Cornflake House porch, it was with less caution and more enthusiasm than at the bus stop. An even stronger seal. We were a pair, boyfriend and girlfriend, and although I was delirious with joy I didn't think I was kidding myself when I saw a dim reflection of my own pleasure in his eyes.

To everyone's surprise we stayed together for weeks, which looked like stretching to months. People began to talk of Marcus and Eve, a pairing which never ceased to lift my heart. I made him laugh, I flattered him, teased him, and paid for him. I also cooked experimental snacks to fill his ever hungry gut and let him fumble about in the dark caravan in a way that was just as experimental as my cooking but far more satisfying. Then, as if the god of wrath himself had picked me out, my glands flared up, filling my throat with pain, making my head throb and my heart break. I knew it was hopeless. Depression is one of the symptoms of that illness, but knowing Marcus wouldn't hang about, faithfully waiting for my recovery, was more sense than sadness. Regardless of this knowledge, I lay with my head back, exposing my lumpy neck to the spring breezes, listening intently for a knock on our door, for his voice in the hall and the sound of my mother's footsteps leading him up to see me.

He never came. I had to gather information from my sisters, an exhausting process involving many questions and not nearly enough answers. Perdita fancied Marcus herself, although she was much too young. She was happy to watch out for him but less willing to relate her findings. I wanted to box her ears or shake her unsullied head, to swap her thoughts about until she gave me some consideration. Zulema was reluctant but reliable, she couldn't help telling the truth, when pressed. She told me what I needed to know but didn't want to hear. Marcus was leading another down lovers' lane while I lay pale and poorly. How could I ever have imagined that pale and poorly was what would appeal to him?

Hence, as I began to recover, the holiday. Two weeks for two people in sunny Spain.

'Please leave Merry and Django behind,' I begged when Mum said she was putting the spending money, part of her prize, towards taking some of the others with us. It was still a lot to ask of Taff, a fortnight babysitting a pair of awkward boys, one bloodyminded girl – Perdita was to stay at home – cats, dogs, small mammals and of course, Cecil the horse. All credit to her, Taff rallied round, arriving a couple of days before we departed 'to get the feel of the job'. She brought with her enough clothes to cover a football pitch and a man called Steve who instantly endeared himself by giving me magic-carpet rides. The floor of the bedroom I shared with my sisters was by then covered in green and yellow lino. The Axminster, upstairs, had suffered enough, having been singed by an electric fire, sicked on, peed on and shaved (don't ask), it was finally pulled up and turfed out.

'You're never too old for a whiz round the lino,' Steve promised as he sat me on a rug and tobogganed me in and out of the spaces between the beds. He was not wrong.

It may well have been my last fling as a child, and I loved it. I'd been cooped up and sorry for myself for so long that my laughter came back like an old friend.

Needless to say, those who stayed in The Cornflake House with Taff and Steve had a far better time than we who packed and left. In Spain, Samik proved once and for all that half his blood was Eskimo and heat didn't agree with him. His skin erupted in tiny, blistering spots, his appetite vanished and his bowels exploded. Since we were squashed into one small room, the rest of us had to tip-toe about while the poor lad tried to sleep through his itching and aching. Fabian, usually starved of the company of girls who looked remotely like himself, fell heavily for a lass from Birmingham, but since she was also sharing a cupboard with her family they were obliged to do their snogging on a beach covered in rubbish and sandflies. And he missed his guitar, having eventually found somebody worth serenading.

Mum spent hours staring at the walls, trying to 'see' how things were going back home.

'Taff's drunk,' she told me, and a hiccup escaped from her chest.

'How about the kids?' this from a girl of fourteen; but then I considered myself a woman, after all hadn't I already loved and lost?

'They're tipsy too. Except Perdita.'

'That figures.'

'No, I mean Perdita isn't merely tipsy, she's out cold. Here, feel my hand.'

I obeyed. It was icy. The image of my sister staggering, dishevelled, possibly even vomiting before she fell, acted like alcohol on me, flowing warmly through my mind. Most of the time, though, I was miserable. It was too soon, my glands hadn't quite settled down, and my heart was still at the raw, stinging stage. Which left Zulema to wander the streets of the little town alone, buying bright presents for her brothers, sending postcards to everyone she knew or had ever known.

That was my holiday. Two weeks with a sick kid and a psychic mother. I did try the brave new world beyond our cramped room but the sun hurt my eyes and even the most bronzed and beautiful boys paled by comparison to my Marcus. When I got back to England, hungry for one kind glance, the bugger couldn't bring himself to face me. He took to using his back door. I'd see him sneaking out, clambering over the hedge at the bottom of his garden, snagging his cord Levi's on brambles. Serve him right.

Mind you, during our fortnight's absence, Taff had transformed The Cornflake House into a shrine to bad taste. There was cut glass everywhere, great ugly bowls on tables, shelves blessed with shimmering vases, swans floating over the window sills. The toilet roll was hidden under the knitted skirts of a 'Victorian' doll, the butter lay buried beneath a Chinese version of Anne Hathaway's cottage. Our first, welcome, cup of tea was poured from a giant pink and silver pot which rested on a set of lion's feet. She'd painted our scruffy old kitchen chairs gold and re-covered them with purple brocade, making it feel, when we parked our weary behinds, as if we'd entered a nursery-rhyme world. I gave an audible sigh and got a scowl from my mother in return. For a second I was glad Marcus had ditched me; I could never have let him see my place like this.

In his own, less offensive way Steve had worked miracles too. Merry was worn out, I kid you not. The child was exhausted from days of football, cricket, horse-walking, swimming and of course magic-carpet rides. Django was engrossed in an entirely new collection of vacuum cleaner catalogues, while Perdita had been taught how to play chess, a game that obsesses her to this day. I ask you, who had the better holiday?

Now, all these years later, I need another chance to find out what drives folk to leave their comfortable homes and fly in silver machines to distant places. Please Matthew, let me sit on warm sand with a whole heart this time. If you don't want me, try not to say so until . . . well, try not to say so. I have my frog nearby. I rubbed my bruises with him, when they hurt like hell, to see if he was magic and could heal. No luck, but the comfort of holding him tight in my fist is indescribable.

You know, in a bizarre way I'll be glad when the day comes. You wouldn't think a woman waiting to be tried for one crime she didn't commit and one she most certainly did could be bored, would you? If I'm not exactly bored, then I am restless. Thank God I've got these letters and the memories they allow. As I'm no longer capable of leaping around the netball court with my fellow prisoners and since I never achieved the honour of working in the laundry like my lucky pal Liz, I'm grateful to be using some of my brain cells at least.

Ten

My life has gone into fast forward. I have frequent meetings with Valerie while we try to think of some way of proving my innocence, and fail. The evidence for half of the crimes of which I'm accused was more than plain for all to see. Although this was intended at the time, it leaves no room now for pretence. Valerie sighs often and has taken to chewing her bottom lip, while I've developed a quiver in my hands and a habit of swinging my left leg. I hit my solicitor's feet under our table several times but she was engrossed in the law and barely noticed. I'm instructed to sit quietly in court, not to mutter under my breath when the police give their account of what happened, and to speak clearly when my turn comes. It has also been hinted that I should chop off my locks, or at least tie them back so that my pale face can shine across at the judge. My hair was used to get me to the floor in my attack. I don't think I'd miss it, not if I'm to spend much more of my life inside. I'll leave it to you, Matthew, will it stay or will it tumble? No, on second thoughts I'll pin it up, the word tumble brings frightening images to mind. Scenes from the film of *A Tale of Two Cities* have begun to flash in my head. An overactive brain is no friend in times of crisis, believe me.

I had another visit from Bing. He appeared to have shrunk, I had to scour the Visitors' Room to find him hunched in his chair. He's been evicted from his hole, a painful business – emotionally and physically. He hardly spoke and his eyes roved around the room longingly. I don't think he'd sat on a chair since his last visit here. In our mutual silence, once he'd raised his eyebrows at my still bruised face, I was compelled to face the fact that I've made my only son homeless. Possibly even motherless, to all extents. What *have* I provided for him? Not security, that's for sure. In a feeble attempt to make good, I suggested he might go and stay with his Uncle Samik for a while. There's a bond between those two which holds tight in spite of Margaret, Samik's boring, possessive wife.

It wasn't surprising that my youngest brother should marry and raise a family – he has four children, all of whom he adores – but none of us expected Margaret. She's as straight as a bowling alley, has no conversation and collects, wait for it, porcelain dolls. Dolls of all sizes and in a great variety of costumes, but mostly sporting frilly bloomers. Their painted faces stare at you from glass cupboards, pouting, smiling inanely, begging for freedom. A visit to Samik's semi, on an estate just outside Guildford, is like going to a museum full of shrunken, stuffed people.

I know why Samik settled down while the rest of us raved and partied. Not being able to have a father, he did the next best thing and became one himself. But I think he went to unnecessary extremes in marrying Margaret. She was faintly pretty until it stopped mattering, now she is more nondescript than plain, with the dress sense of a three-year-old let loose in her mother's wardrobe. Old-fashioned? Well, not if you like half-pleated skirts and twin-sets. And Margaret hides a heart of granite behind those pearly buttons. She can be tough, stubborn, immutable, but never passionate, which is what makes her so tedious. Whereas Samik is a beautiful man with a sweet nature; he could have done much better. I'm never sure if he sees it that way himself, if so he gives no hint. His loyalty to his chosen life seems total. Family and boats, those are his twin preoccupations. He owns two boats, one a floating bar which keeps the lot of them in food and clothing, the other a small yacht moored on the south coast and called – you'll appreciate the irony – Spirit Of Adventure II. Spirit Of Adventure I was destroyed when it ran into a rock.

'Oh yeah?' Fabian mused when told of this catastrophe, 'and what was the rock called? Margaret?'

Before he met his match, Samik was devoted to Bing. I moved back to The Cornflake House while my son was still in nappies. All the love Samik had been storing up was given to his baby nephew. Youngest children do sometimes suffer from not having anybody to mother or father, I suppose. Mum and I sat back, watching as he played with little Blessing, smiling as the baby smiled at the affection in the eyes of the young uncle. It's fair to say that Samik was a substitute father for Bing, even to the point of leaving when my son was growing and most in need of a man in his life. It might be guilt which encourages Samik to make room for his crusty nephew when there is clearly no space left for anybody else. For whatever reason, I know that if Bing tramps or hitches to Guildford, he'll find a welcome at his uncle's house. Maybe only half a welcome; Margaret has no sympathy with Bing, she thinks he should be a fully-trained computer programmer by now.

Being a brave soul, not afraid of dark places, my son promised he would get himself to Samik's for a break.

'Will you be all right?' Bing asked me, his voice slurred with lack of sleep and the effort of asking an almost emotional question. How should I know? I could be far from hunky bloody dory by this time next week, not that I'm exactly floating in ecstasy now. I could be banged up, locked away, doomed to suffer not one but an endless stream of attacks from bullies. My eyes might pop out altogether, my lips swell like melons. How was I supposed to answer Bing?

'Yes,' ever the coward, avoiding eye contact, 'I'll be fine. Got a wonderful solicitor, female, very caring.' God, if he only knew, he wouldn't trust Valerie to get him off a charge in Woking had he been in Australia at the time of the crime.

I'll have to try harder, if I'm released. Have to find some-where for him to think of as home. Being locked up has wakened maternal feelings which have lain rather dormant for the past few years. I watched Bing leaving with a terrible sinking of my heart, a mixture of love, regret, and guilt.

I've become famous, notorious, in my own social circle. On my rare trips to the Visitors' Room, voices drop at my entrance, whispers hiss from the lips of other prisoners. 'That's her,' they say, urgently, 'that's the one who killed her mother.' My fame encompasses those who visit me, being a friend or relation to such evil singles people out. Not that Bing needs any help there, he looks exceptional enough, God knows; and as for Merry, well he'd stand out, even if he managed to stand still, at any gathering. But you must have found your back burning from the stares and glares, haven't you, Matthew? I'd rather be on my own than put you through that humiliation. That's part of the reason why I'm going to ask you not to come to my trial. The other part is that it's important for me to keep something separate, to have a person I care about who isn't involved in the past, the trial, the whole mess. I'm not playing the heroine, the martyr who prefers to stand alone in Joan of Arcish glory, I only want you waiting in the wings instead of on stage witnessing the tremors. Does it make sense? Sense being a tad elusive these days, I really have no idea.

Odd that I choose to stand alone. Until my mother died I'd never been alone. I'd always known there was one person who cared unquestioningly about me and my welfare. Do you believe in soulmates? I certainly do. For each of us there has to be another, a twin of the heart. Most individuals find this person through romantic love, don't they? Once they've fled the nest they substitute lover for mother, or father. Not in my case, until now. Maybe Mum's magic did outlive her, otherwise how can I account for the way you turned up just as her curtain fell?

My jealously of Taff is based here, somewhere. She was more than an ordinary friend to Victory. As I said, I didn't get around to making friends in my earlier life (I think of life as divided in two, neatly sliced down the middle by the death of my mother). It's true that Taff took lover after lover, but it was in Mum's company that she shone brightest. And, if I'm woman enough to admit it, Mum was happiest, most alive when that silly lemon-on-legs came to visit. It has to be said that they were good together, once they got going their humour was a game of tennis, jokes bouncing from player to player with us kids turning our heads to watch for the next shot. They joked on most subjects, twisting everything in blazing innuendos:

(Television)

'It's all a load of crap, in't it?'

'Well you don't have to watch it. You can always turn the knob.'

'You know me, Darling, just show me a knob worth turning . . .'

(Knitting. Taff knitted extraordinary objects on vast needles, using fluffy day-glow wools of shocking pink and orange, mixed.)

'Whoops, I've made a boob.'

'Can't see why. You've got two perfectly good ones already.'

(Dancing)

'I'm learning proper dancing, Vic.'

'Ballroom?'

'Only if I really fancy me partner.'

Mum and Taff would go for weeks without contact, months even when we were little and time consuming but, the second they screeched into each other's arms, their friendship resumed exactly where it had left off. I've had lovers who mattered a great deal to me but the seat on the top of my pedestal was always taken. Being the first-born, I felt it only right I should be the apple of Mum's eye. It didn't occur to me to be envious of my brothers and sisters, they were loved and protected as was to be expected, but they would never push me from the front of the queue. It was only when Taff came by, or telephoned for hours on end, and Mum's face lit with undisguised delight, that jealousy gnawed inside me.

Well I outwitted Taff at the end. It was me Mum turned to in her final hours, me she trusted. Taff wouldn't have done it. She might have said 'Yes, all right,' but when the moment came her courage would've failed. Unlike mine. Paying this price is small punishment compared to how I might have felt about being passed over in favour of Taff. You see I understood the history behind Mum's request. I knew that she believed there was a circle to be completed. From my cradle I'd been told of the beginnings of this circle, I had lived the centre part all my life, and I alone could be relied on to tie the ends together.

I have quite a stack of post now, my frog has become a paperweight, but the letter from Taff remains unopened. I won't give her the satisfaction.

Can I use you as a sounding board? I know I wrote to Valerie and she's read that account of the final night, but I've not been able to talk about the months before my mother's death. Nobody can lend an ear the way you do.

I should go back further first, to the missing years. The Cornflake House was never empty. One by one the children left home – only I returned for good – but between them my brothers and sisters kept up a constant stream of visits. Also Mum became quite famous as a clairvoyant and a healer. She didn't advertise, word got around from one satisfied customer to another. Hopeful 'clients' trudged up the path, their legs brushed by our overgrown grass, their eyes drawn to the ancient caravan. After half an hour with Victory, they'd practically skip back to their cars. Many of these believers crossed her palm with silver. I heard the tinkling of coins.

In fact I waited discreetly for this cue before knocking and offering mugs of tea or coffee. Generous customers caused a breakdown in this system by handing Mum a note or two, so she developed a gentle cough as a signal. This went on for years. Of course I wasn't always there, I often worked. Mum had insisted I use my brain; she was so proud of my being able to read and write well that she kept me hard at my studies until I qualified to teach. Not having been happy at school myself, I found it hard to commit to spending hours in class or common rooms. I either taught kids in their homes or did supply teaching in bursts for as long as I could stand it. I had a live-in childminder in Mum, making me luckier than most single parents.

While I worked and Mum healed, little Blessing was growing up to all the prejudice I'd had to face before him, a bastard, poor as a tramp, in an area of tennis courts and rhododendrons. His heritage was disapproval. Following in the footsteps of The Cornflake House kids, in good old Fisher's Close, can't have been easy. I'll give you an example from my own childhood, you'll have to take a backwards leap to keep up, but you did ask what it was like, living there, being me.

I imagine astronauts feel as we did, light-headed, other-worldly, select and proud of it, but troubled. When we moved to Fisher's Close age suddenly made a difference. At Grandma's we'd all run around together, playing, fighting, being kids. But in Surrey you had to be very young not to notice the condemnation of our neighbours, not to mind the pursed mouths. I mean it was one thing to be me, eight years old with four years of schooling to my credit, and quite another to be a toddler like Merry. I know, that's a bad example. Merry was the same at eight, and at eighteen, as he was when wearing romper suits.

We'd been given this jewel, this treasure, literally a prize most could only dream of; but in true fairy-tale tradition, the precious gift brought its own limitations. We loved The Cornflake House, it was what we'd always wanted, a home of our own, miles from the bitter east wind, far from Grandad Eric and his stick. The place was new, ours to furnish with belongings, to decorate with scribblings, to fill with smells and sounds. It had a garden and two toilets; who could ask for more? And we were far from ungrateful or unappreciative. We were determined to enjoy it, to belong to it. I think we succeeded; at least indoors we managed to feel that we'd arrived, that we were home. But outside, what could we do? Even without our untrained dogs and our murderous cats, even if we'd been neater, quieter children, the sheer volume of our family, the colours of our skins and Mum's single-parent status would have set us apart.

I remember one day, during the Christmas holidays, when it snowed. I woke to find the room transformed into a cave surrounded by mystical light. I'd seen snow before, but not here, heaped against this window, inviting me out. The world was a child's heaven, roofs were giant slides, trees had been covered in cotton-wool and cars were rounded and white, drawings waiting to be coloured in. The pure, untrodden ground called to me. For once I was entirely selfish. I dressed silently, not waking my sisters, and tip-toed from the bedroom in my thick socks. I knew that later there'd be snowball fights, and seven of us making a great grinning snowman. We'd take trays to the slopes on the golf course, compacting the snow until we could race downhill with our legs in the air. Low branches of trees would be shaken, covering us with falls of freezing snow, gloves would go soggy, noses run. Later we'd enjoy this together. First I wanted to own the hushed, white world, to tread softly, making the first footprints, to be a fallen angel on a fresh, white lawn. One rush of icy, exhilarating air as I opened the door and I was outside, alone while the others slept.

I walked as lightly as I could in wellingtons, drawing patterns with my feet. When I did my fallen angel, I let my body collapse backwards, then rubbed my arms gently up and down on the snow to make the shape of wings. I was trying to get up carefully, not wanting to spoil the image, when a shadow fell across me. First I saw the shovel, a chunk of metal between my splayed legs, then I recognized Mr Powell, father of the dreaded Fiona, looking down on me. He offered his hand and I let him pull me to my feet.

'You kids,' he complained, 'there's always one of you in trouble, falling over, messing about, isn't there?' I felt ashamed, reduced to a red-faced girl when moments before I'd been The Angel Of The Snow. Mr Powell told me to get on inside and dry myself before I caught my death. He then proceeded to scrape the clean, beautiful snow from our path, leaving our garden with a mess of sludge and a spaghetti junction of footprints as he did us this favour.

That was the outdoor terrain, while inside there was a warm, extremely loving woman whose life was seeped in beliefs and superstitions. A womb of a house in which one never wore green clothing, or passed another on the stairs, where knives on floors meant visitors were on the way; and as long as you flung any spilt salt over your shoulder, all would always be well. A place far removed from the offices, restaurants and banks of the Mr Powells of this world.

Years later, enter Bing, a child with an adoring grand-mother and a fairly keen mother, but, like his uncles and aunts, fatherless and, unlike them, an only child. It had been easier for me. I'd had my brothers and sisters to protect, most of them more obvious fuel for bullying than me, and I'd happily been their warrior, fighting battles either for or with them. But Blessing was singled out and taken to pieces without anybody to help or support him. We kept a good supply of Witch Hazel in The Cornflake House when Bing was small. Mum and I were often to be seen marching down the school drive, scowls set on our faces, ready to sort whoever needed sorting. In the end Bing solved the problem himself. By the time he reached secondary school he was so laid back that nobody could see the point of bothering him. Harsh words bounced off him like balls against a wall. Unfor-tunately most of his lessons also bounced away into a forgotten distance. He left school uneducated in everything but survival. It's not surprising he's taken to activities where that talent comes in handy.

During those years I dated many men. Some were of the check-shirt variety, schoolmasters, with inky fingers and pipe-stained teeth. A few were hippies, gentle folk breezing through Surrey on their way across Europe, staying with us for a week or a month before the road called and they ignited their camper vans, jolting off to catch a ferry. Mum provided good food, fascinating conversation and gallons of hot water in which they might wash themselves and their smelly socks. I met these elusive beings at festivals or in jazz clubs, doing well at the game of picking up. It was contrast that attracted men to me. I was in a black phase then. Drop your eyes to the ground and you'll see black suede shoes, black tights, travel up to a short, straight black skirt and on to the equally inky polo-neck sweater, but then onwards to a white face, caked in the palest make-up, and lastly, above it all a crown of long, waving, golden hair. The swarthy opposed to the milky, ebony and gold. It worked every time.

In schools I was considered an interesting oddity, not only because of my clothing. I wore a great deal of musky perfume and painted my fingernails alternately silver and black. Because I was heavily into wholefoods, the gaps between my teeth were always full of seeds which I attacked absent-mindedly throughout the day.

That's me then, well loved, with an identity I liked, having plenty of sex and nourished by goodly grains. Mum seemed contented too. She'd raised her family but hadn't been abandoned entirely. Her love for Blessing was a constant reminder to me of the joy she gave to children; a reminder which made me appreciate that *I* was the one who'd been truly blessed. We were in the happy position of being able to repeat childhood highlights; taking Blessing on picnics to woods we'd visited years before, reliving old Christmases as he ripped paper from presents, reading him bedtime stories that had been loved by his aunts and uncles.

Once the pressure was off and her own children grown, Mum became relaxed about her magic, more ready to experiment. With my generation she'd been careful, never doing anything out of the ordinary when the ordinary would suffice; but Blessing was treated to special showings of tricks which would have made the average conjurer give up and take to selling insurance. I was on the porch once, saying goodnight to a date, when the lights in The Cornflake House began to flash. Not haphazardly as in a storm, but rhythmically like Christmas-tree lights, one on then off, another the same, then all off, all on, upstairs only, downstairs only. It was dizzying, mesmeric. I pulled my young man's hand and led him backwards until we stood not far from Marcus's house, watching the garden fall under small spotlights. Now you see the caravan, now the tree.

'Hadn't you better call somebody out?' my lover asked.

I looked at him without comprehension. Did he want me to get Mum outside, to view her show from this angle?

'You ought to call the Electricity Board. It looks dangerous to me.'

Not a surprising response, I grant you, but dull enough to send me on that sudden fall which hurtles one out of love.

'Never be afraid of electricity,' Mum advised me not long afterwards, 'it'll not harm you.' And she clicked her fingers at the kettle which began to boil obediently. If we used the electric chair in this country, I might be finding comfort in those words today.

I had an inkling about electricity anyway, just as I am absolutely at ease in motor cars or on buses. My end will not come that way, violently on road or motorway. Understandably I shrink from discovering how it *will* come, foresight has to be controlled to be enjoyed, but the shadow of death moves quietly over my head. It was the same for Mum, except she knew not only how it wouldn't be, but how it would. She was braver than I, and had faced the scene of her death many times before it happened. Magic and death; as I said, the two are bound together.

Forebodings of death were shared experiences for us. I

remember my knees turning to jelly and my heart aching when I was at school.

'I have to go home,' I told my teacher, 'now.' Not waiting for permission, I ran to the bus stop and paced restlessly until the sixty-three ambled along. Did I know what was wrong? Or only that something had happened? I can't be sure; I was young, afraid, frustrated by the torturous progress of that blasted bus. By the time I reached my stop I was in tears, my head throbbing as if the sea had invaded my skull. Mum was on the front lawn, her head lifted like an animal trying to place a scent. She opened her arms for me and stroked my hair.

'I think it's your Grandad,' she told me, 'the lamp fell off the mantelpiece, but I knew anyway. We'll go inside and wait.'

There were telegrams in those days, missives of congratulations or doom. Ours came about an hour later. Eric had died; Editha wanted Mum to go immediately. I cried, maybe more for my Grandma than for the departed, but my mother only bit her lip and worried about leaving us.

'Where is Taff now,' she asked herself, 'she said she was going to London, but when? She won't mind, at a time like this, wherever she is.'

Luckily there weren't many repetitions of this joint knowledge of impending death. Grandma Editha died in The Cornflake House, and *everybody* who lived there saw that end coming, including Grandma herself.

Mum did some amazing things in those between years. Not just displays to delight her grandson but, as I said, a great deal of fortune-telling and healing. She mixed and matched these talents. People who came to discover whether they were about to meet Mr or Mrs Right often found themselves being cured of aches and pains at no extra cost. Mum could sense pain from across the room; 'You've had a lot of trouble with your back, have you?' she'd ask unsuspecting visitors as they sipped their after-session tea. 'Come here and sit in front of me.' Then she would touch the trouble spot, gently. Her hands were warm when healing, not lukewarm, more the temperature of the average hot-water bottle. Pain bowed out under the mild pressure of those hands. I experienced that touch several times and nothing in the world compares with it. The blood would tingle in my veins, the skin on my scalp would tighten as a warm sensation flowed through every part of me. While I felt my headache clear, I knew the true meaning of the word luxury, for my mother's method of healing was a salve to body and spirit.

Sadly I learnt, too late, that every time she laid her hands on another soul, Mum's own energy was decreasing.

I doubt if even you can imagine how I felt when I came to understand this. Alone in a room I'd once shared, I sat and cried long, quiet tears for her, and for myself. Every time she'd helped me, each magical demonstration for Blessing, the competitions and the fun, the healing, all these had taken their toll. Without saying a word, she'd known this was so, and carried on using her fatal talent. By the time I could act, it was too late. My mother was dying.

I put a sign on the front door, 'Victory can see nobody', then I pulled the bolt for good measure. Only family were allowed inside. As hopeful clients shuffled back down our path, I'd sigh with relief, but Mum felt their disappointment deeply in the very part of her which was ailing from previously helping them. I had to rise early and stay up late to perform the task of sentry. People in need have no respect for the sick, they'd ring our bell at all hours. Once, and only once, one of Mum's regulars caught me out. I came down the stairs at six in the morning to find Mum sitting opposite this woman, her face ashen, eyes closed. Exhausted. The visitor was marched out: there are some advantages to being well-built.

We were cosy and companionable in those closing months. In the evenings, when I looked across the room and smiled at Mum who'd be sneaking a glance at me, I understood the expression 'broken-hearted'. The ache I lived with was centred in my breast, often giving the impression that the organ which kept me alive was in the process of slowly cracking. Do you see me bravely carrying on as if all was well? Hiding my sorrow? If so, switch pictures. This was my mother, my heart and soul, I could hide nothing from her. She comforted me, when it should have been the other way around; 'Things'll work out for you, Evey,' she promised as I soaked her shoulder.

'I don't see how, without you.'

'No, I wouldn't expect you to see, but try and believe.'

Was it you, Matthew? Were you the one I was supposed to believe in? Or did she mean the trial? Maybe she knew I would suffer prison, attacks, loneliness, love-sickness, and triumph over these afflictions. Shall I be stronger for it, more able to live without her? You see, even now, at the lowest ebb, I do believe in magic, her magic. I panic, but I have an inherent seam of hope. She was a clever woman, my mother. Not educated, not able to read or write easily, but with a given instinct and an intelligence capable of planning beyond the grave.

An enormous rock is falling into place. My God, she made me do it for myself as well as for her peace of mind. What would I have done if I *hadn't* come to prison? How was I supposed to handle her funeral, booking the church, flowers, a hearse, while my mind was wild with grief? She thought the whole thing through, organizing the worst days of my life so that they'd be frenzied enough to take my mind off the shattering sadness of losing her. Putting me safely out of harm's way, beyond pills or knives or ravines, or at least ensuring I was watched over, until ... until you came to rescue me. Sorry my love, but you are part of *this* life's rich pattern; we have been woven into place by an expert in colour, texture, composition.

I'm crying again. A benign shadow nods her approval; 'You may be bright, but you're slower than a slug through mud, Evey.'

If you knew how I miss her – my arms are empty, aching for a hug.

Will you touch me? When next we meet, for the last time before my trial, will you reach over and hold my hand? I know it's allowed, I've seen dads, husbands, lovers make this gesture. Recently I've been searched and attacked, those are my physical experiences. I haven't been touched tenderly since my mother squeezed my hand, closed her eyes and slipped from this world.

I didn't kill her, Matthew. I must share that responsibility with everybody who grasped any part of her powers. Do you think she took *my* talent with her to the grave, saving me from having to suffer the same fate as herself? I wonder if

Zulema has also lost the ability to foresee events, to change things. Did Mum bestow these gifts on us, perhaps? I assumed they were inherited, but now I'm not so sure. If given, they could be retracted. I appreciate that death entails a loss of energy, but at the moment of her death, my mother sighed as if she had nothing left; as if crushed by rocks. Was that because she consumed all the magic in our family? I'll never know. My only comfort is that I gave her peace of mind, before and after her dying.

The problem is this; the rest of the world can't see what happened as a balm, a relieving, freeing action. I had to be destructive to be constructive. Come with me on this journey of baptism if you dare. There's no going back; once I've led you through fire, we will be joined for life.

Are you still there, Matthew? Do I see you with a hand outstretched, waiting for me?

I love you.

How could I take you through hell if this was mere infatuation? I would only show my poor, dead mother to the man I love. Look at her, grey ringlets laid on her pillow, mouth set in a wistful smile, taking secrets to the other side. I bend and kiss her cheek, inhaling the smell of her skin. Should I cover her face? My hand is shaking, I drop the counterpane before it reaches her chin. She wouldn't have hidden in life, she shall 'see' it through to the end. I have to cling to the banister as I go down the stairs. I turn on the kitchen tap and gulp cold water from my hands, splashing my face, mixing tears and drink together. Then I hear her voice. Oh I don't jump, I know it's a ghost, and a loving one at that. She encourages me, calms me. I do what has to be done automatically after this, one action following another, just as we planned.

My surroundings are so familiar that I do none of the final looking about, taking in everything for the last time. In fact I hardly notice where I am until I stand outside in the garden. Then I gaze at The Cornflake House as if seeing it for the first time. As if Owen has only just brought me here, to this prize.

My mother loved Surrey. After the fens she found the gentle slopes refreshing. 'Leafy Surrey', with its silver birch and tall, fat pine trees. She liked to pull the tips off bracken, when it was new and moist, and rub these between her fingers until her skin was green and smelt of spring. Even the heaths, frustratingly difficult to walk with their gorse bushes and tufts of heather, were pleasure grounds to her. Mum never wore trousers, she favoured full skirts – perhaps in order to look the Gypsy – and on Walking Days these swung about her legs above a pair of clumsy hiking boots. But she always took care not to tread on wild flowers, small animals, even spiders. Nothing in nature frightened her, not rats, not snakes, not insects that sting or bite. We children grew up accepting all creatures, from humans down to ants.

As I stood and stared at The Cornflake House on the day of my mother's death, I saw how nature had navigated around the minor setback of Fisher's Close, and how we'd provided an oasis for butterflies and bees in a desert of clipped lawns and trim flower beds. It was a sight, our house, paint chipped, windows cracked, curtains hanging at odd angles; but it was more at home with the tall trees behind the little estate, more at peace with the ferns and hawthorns than any of its companions. Perhaps if we'd bought it, paying good money for the privilege of living tidily, we might have kept the place in better repair. Maybe if there'd been a man about the house ... On the other hand, my mother had a purpose in all she did and all she left undone. Knowing what she was to ask of me, she'd probably intended to let the house go partially to ruin.

Don't be afraid. I've already set free the last of the birds. There are no dogs left alive, and the cats are in the woods behind the houses, chasing poor fledglings. You won't hear any squarks or whines. We must hurry. Death has a way of attracting attention and we don't want our neighbours coming round, sniffing about, asking questions. Everything we need is in the caravan, which doubles as a garden shed. This is the risky bit, carrying these cans up to the house without being noticed. Do you think three is enough? It had to be either three or seven, Mum insisted. Numbers, she was so sure of their power. To speak, to think of her in the past tense, I can't believe ... Bless her for giving me this task, to keep me occupied. She was right, it feels the right thing to do, doesn't it? Terrible yet wonderful. Passionate.

I'll take the upstairs, it's my responsibility and I know what to do. In my mind I've carried these cans, their contents splashing, that smell escaping through sealed tops, a hundred times. But nothing prepared me for the real thing, for the sound, almost comical, of metal banging the stairs, of my breathing as I heave the blasted can, of my nails as they rip to shreds while struggling with the clasp. Considering the age I live in, I've spent exceptionally little time in motor cars. The fumes catch me unawares, filling my eyes, making me cough. Half the contents, one sixth of the total, ends up on the landing as I tip too violently. My right hand is soaked and I leave the can and tip-toe into my mother's bedroom. I anoint her forehead with the liquid, not making a sign but stroking her brow, feeling her skin move under my fingers, across her skull.

From then on I move like the wind, before nerves overcome me. The rest of the petrol is poured, scattered haphazardly here and there. The stink is unbearable now, I'm worried it will drift to next door, to the other houses. Leaving the front door open, I exit, taking three backwards steps, stumbling over a pile of papers, holding the long taper in one hand, the matches in the other. Fumbling, trembling, I pull out a match and place the taper in my teeth. I have both hands free to strike. I do this quickly, dropping the box of matches to the ground as soon as my chosen one ignites. The flame touches the taper. The taper touches the petrol-drenched papers in the hall. The Cornflake House roars. It is done.

Eleven

Yes, it was done. I wonder if my mother ever doubted me? If so there was no need; it never occurred to me not to obey. Had she asked me to walk through the fire, I wouldn't be here, telling my tale.

Tears streamed down my cheeks as I stood watching The Cornflake House burn. That old song's right enough, smoke does get in your eyes, and up your nose. I smelt of it for weeks, as if I was made of ash. Can you imagine how bright a house on fire can be, how much heat it gives off? I'd invented a million monsters, flames sprang from nowhere, breeding more flames. Once created they were instantly vast, eternally hungry. They devoured everything, furniture, floors, curtains, the worn Axminster. And upstairs, the body on the bed, the corpse for cremation. I thought nonsense, Ladybird, Ladybird fly away home . . . nonsense. Anything to keep my feet planted on the spot, to stop me from running back to my home, to rescue treasures; to carry my mother to safety. Then I wished the fire brigade shouldn't come soon. The image of my mother's corpse, charred and hanging over a man's shoulder, danced in the haze before my eyes. Too terrible.

I was limp with heat, scarlet on the outside, melting beneath my skin. How mad I must have looked. A demented soul on the edge of hell.

When did I come to my senses? Was it as the first frantic neighbour pulled me back, away from the heat? Or later, when the authorities arrived, one emergency service screaming on the heels of the next, in Ealing Comedy fashion? Did I recover? Will I ever be over the shock?

'Is there anybody in there?' a fireman yelled, his hose and mask at the ready.

'My mother,' I said. I'm sure I added, 'but she's dead, don't rescue her, she's dead'. No, I'm not sure. My only clear memory is that of being wrapped in a blanket, a kindness which brought me to the brink of hysterics. A blanket, in that heat; never mind coals to Newcastle, this was taking an electric fire to the sun. But later, when they tried to take the blanket back, I became possessive, pulling it tightly round my shoulders. I suppose I was coming to realize that I had nothing left, nothing of my own. Homeless people grow attached to their blankets, I fully understand why.

To begin with everbody was very kind. An ambulance man told me to let myself go. 'Have a good howl, Love,' he advised, 'nothing like a flow of tears to help get over shock.' I expect I stared at him as if he'd just arrived from Mars. They seemed to be giants, green giants, yellow plastic giants, joke policemen and women looming yards above my head. The faces of the yellow-plastic-fireman giants changed from white to black as they emerged from the rubble that had been my house. Colour wasn't the only change. The light of sympathy, which had been glowing behind the look of efficiency, had gone from their eyes. With the first whiff of petrol, I switched from victim to criminal. From where I sat, in the open back door of an ambulance, it sounded like a load of kids swearing; 'Arson. Arson. Arson.'

'Your house?' a policeman asked. I expect I nodded. I may even have smiled sadly, there being so little left of 'my house'. It was a sorry sight, an oversized bonfire sending clouds of black smoke into a spring evening sky. Hissing in protest, stinking fit to choke a body.

'Only there's talk of petrol,' the policeman explained, 'which means an investigation, questions, d'you see?' I saw little, understood nothing.

'Somebody said your mother was in there,' my persistent policeman told me. 'Is that right?'

'She's dead.'

'Yes, well,' he shuffled his ash-covered feet, 'I'm sorry. But was she alive when it started?'

I dare say there's a transcript in an office with my answer. If I gave one.

It was at this point that a sooty-faced fireman appeared with Zulema's moon pendant in his gloved hand. I thought it was an offering and reached for it, but he closed his fist saying, as parents say to small children, 'Hot.'

I suppose he must have kept it.

What followed was a polite battle. Everybody wanted me to themselves. The ambulance folk were certain I should be leaving with them, the police said no, I was uninjured and could ride in their gleaming white vehicle. At one time I was having my left arm pulled in one direction, my right in the other. Or so it felt. I was light-headed, practically stoned on the smell of smoke and decay. The people from the hospital wanted to treat me for shock; but what's the cure for death followed by fire? Had I been a true pyromaniac I'd no doubt have been lapping up the attention; I was certainly at the centre of this, for the time being. The inhabitants of Fisher's Close had left their bridge parties and tottered out, some with whisky glasses clenched in their fists, to view the downfall of The Cornflake House with what must have been mixed emotions. I'm sure they were glad it had gone, but then there was this mess to be cleared before another, proper family could build on the site. So there was quite a crowd around me that evening as I stood in our smouldering clearing praying that my mother had vanished, bones and all.

Valerie thought we might try saying that I was entranced when I set fire to the house. She thought this could work, because of Mum's reputation as a fortune-teller and healer.

'But not as a hypnotist,' I pointed out. Of course I knew perfectly well that Mum used thought transference many times, but I also understood that I'd done the dreaded deed while in full possession of my senses. It was only later, once the flames bit and blackened and put on a fine show of their dexterity, that I became mesmerized. Valerie's only hope lies in the fact that I was driven close to madness by my actions. There'll be little enough logic in the police reports. By the time I reached the interview room, exhaustion and deep shock had silenced me. Grief only added to my dumbness as I sat on that hard chair shivering, a child wanting its mother.

I have wondered, in spite of all I've said about being the loyal, dutiful daughter, whether or not I did the right thing. I'm not convinced that Mum thought it through, that she took the strong arm of the law into consideration when asking me to torch The Cornflake House the moment she died. In retrospect, now that I've had more than enough time to contemplate the full implications of my action, I see that I made my brothers and sisters homeless. Some of them have other homes now, of course, but the house you grow up in, that's the core, isn't it? No matter if we were unpopular in Fisher's Close; we won our home fair and square and built a mountain of memories around the place – like any other family. Have I sentenced them to wander the earth, or to live in semis or huts, without a base for the rest of their days? I'm not talking of inheritance. Lord knows one tatty house, even in such an exclusive cul-de-sac, wouldn't have gone far divided by seven. This isn't about money, only about value. I deprived my family of the thing they valued most.

If only we had fathers, gallant men who could come charging over the horizon now, offering comfort and inheritances.

The more this goes around in my head, the nearer I get to being angry with my mother. It was all very well for her, lying there with that smile on her lips, but what about the living? Didn't she understand that flames obliterate other images? They burn long after firemen extinguish them, leaving only orange in the eye. As time goes on, and my trial draws near, I see The Cornflake House less clearly through the heat haze. By the time I get out of here and have a life to call my own, I doubt if I'll be able to remember the place as anything other than a pile of smouldering cinders.

Would it have mattered if I'd said one thing, and done another? Would it have made any difference to Mum if I'd agreed with her plan, acting my part sincerely until the moment of her death, but then walking downstairs and telephoning a doctor and an undertaker? Stupid even to wonder. I couldn't have fooled her with play-acting, not for a second. Anyway, it's the life after death question again. The trouble is that none of us, in the wake of death, want to believe in its finality. Most of us organize moving services, selecting the departed one's favourite music or poems, in order to please them; because we can't admit that it doesn't matter, that they have gone beyond caring about arrangements. Will they understand in court that I was conforming, in my way, to this common human ritual when I lit the match? That I was in the sorry state of make-believe known only to those who suffer loss? I doubt they'd sympathize. Might as well say the Devil himself visited one night and told me to set fire to my home.

I might be making an ogre of my mother. Do you see her as an unreasonable, bitter woman trying to disinherit her kids and make life after her death as difficult for me as possible? I should be writing on a blackboard, then we could wipe the slate clean. Mum never wanted anything but happiness for her children. Perhaps her view of life was a little lopsided. She saw more than most people in some respects, her vision went beyond their everyday scope. Then again, she looked at life from one standpoint only, taking each issue as it arose and heading for a solution down a tunnel of what she considered right.

'It'll be no good for you, Eve, living on here by yourself,' she told me when there was no denying how ill she was, 'having your brothers and sisters visit, sensing them wanting this and that possession, knowing they were whispering about your right to live in the place while they had to make their own ways.'

What she said made good sense. She presented me with scenes when she spoke. I could actually see Perdita pulling up in a smart motor car, hear her clip-clopping down the path in high-heeled shoes, feel the dampness of her hands as she fingered ornaments she meant to take away with her.

'Besides which,' Mum smiled, 'I like to think of you away from this Close. Getting on with another part of your life, once I'm gone.'

I was torn between remonstrating, asking how could I think of life without her, and spying this future through the cracks in my sorrow. As long as my mother lived, her magic thrived; the image she conjured for me was too strong to ignore. I saw this other part of my life – white houses, crimson wildflowers, sparse shrubs, goats, and further out, when I shielded my eyes, the sea silvered by bright sunlight. A foreign landscape, almost as far removed from The Cornflake House as Zulema's beloved moon.

'It will set you free, Eve,' my mother promised, 'there's nothing like fire for release. The world is peopled with tribes and communities who believe in the power of fire. I believe in it too. Besides, all this,' she waved a hand at the furniture and ornaments, 'this tat. Wouldn't life be easier without it? I give you freedom, a state worth the learning.'

I could see her point, as usual. To be honest I didn't relish living alone in a shrine full of junk.

'Then there's the neighbours,' Mum told me. 'Just as one lot get used to us, another bunch moves in and the snobbery starts over again. It's been fine as a family, uniting forces, turning more than one cheek, but a single woman . . . You'd use up all your strength in the battle, Eve, and grow old and eccentric meanwhile.'

'You see me with a rolling-pin, do you, grey hair flying, hairy dressing-gown flapping about even hairier legs, chasing Little Lord Fauntleroys off my precious patch of garden?'

'I hear cultured voices drifting over the hydrangeas, saying the most hurtful things about you in the nicest possible way. I see you walking through the Close, your outfits getting more daring by the day, your mouth set in resolution but your heart heavy with mistrust. I feel your despair as you grow ever poorer, lonelier and less loved.'

I was there, stuck in the quicksand of that scenario, 'And the house?' I asked. 'How does it fare without you?'

'Not well,' and she raised one eyebrow, 'but then when has it ever? I haven't done a lot for the place, have I? I can hardly be accused of wasting my time with DIY and so on. Still, we kept it bright, between us. Homely. It's always been a dry ship in a safe harbour, eh?'

This was a confusing description, because if the inside of The Cornflake House was reminiscent of anything – other than a jumble sale – it was an old, wooden caravan. My mother had won a characterless, modern house, and transformed it, slowly, lovingly, into a vast Gypsy caravan. I was amused as I looked around at the red walls, the pictures in their painted frames, the brass ornaments winking from every surface. Not a ship in a safe harbour, but a stranded caravan, one that had wandered from the train and become too inflated, too overloaded to return to the road. The egg-caravan in our garden had been the best Mum could manage before her win, but once she'd got something bigger to transform, well, she'd really gone back to what she believed

was her nature. I remembered Cecil the horse, now long
gone to that great pasture in the sky. I didn't doubt Mum's
story of him having been brought to us by some man, but
why, it occurred to me, would this happen? Why the sudden
generosity, even if the man in question was the father of one
of us kids? Because Mum had wanted a horse, that was why.
It seemed likely that, having set her heart on perfecting the
Gypsy image, she'd ordered one, the way folks order sofas
or built-in wardrobes.

As usual, Mum read my mind and we met each other's
eyes, understanding perfectly.

'They may like to burn the lot, Mum,' I said, 'those
Gypsies of yours, caravan, belongings and all, but do they
usually leave the body inside? I don't think so.'

'It's like this,' she told me, 'I want the lot to go up in
smoke, a freeing of the spirit, no possessions left, nothing to
cart around in the hereafter. I want it done straight away,
before the authorities get wind of my death. And I can't be
doing with ceremony, Eve, not church or those poky little
chapels for cremation. I'd burn anyway, Dear, and I'd rather
do so here, where we've been cosy and together, than in a
greasy furnace.'

What could I say? It would have been cruel to deny her;
besides she was right. The local cemetery has been full for
years now, and not being a church-goer, not having booked
a plot, well there'd have been no hope of burial; she'd have
burnt anyway.

There lies the way through the tangle. Valerie should use
this information: my mother was obsessed, from an early
age, with the idea that she was of Gypsy blood. She asked
me to burn her home because that was how it was done, or

used to be done, by the people she believed she came from. I can try to explain, if I'm allowed, how hard it had been, living under the shadow of death with such a strong and single-minded woman.

What a time that was for me, with my mother growing weaker by the day and her impressions of my bleak future in The Cornflake House strengthening. No wonder I took little persuading when it came to destruction; I was an emotional mess, I'd have agreed to anything just to change the subject. On the night she talked of safe harbours I took a deep breath and stepped gingerly on to forbidden ground. I did so in an effort to go backwards, to the past, in order to take our minds off what was to come.

'Will you tell me,' I asked tentatively, 'about the fathers?'

The second the words passed my lips I wished I'd kept my mouth shut. No other question could have brought the situation home to me so clearly. To begin with there was the chance she might answer, and that diversity from the normal lack of willingness to speak of those men would indicate that Mum had reached a turning point; that she considered her death not only inevitable but imminent. That there was nothing left to lose and she might as well take this final opportunity to fill the gaps in my knowledge. On the other hand she could keep quiet, evading answers, as always. But this option made my skin freeze too, because it meant that we, mother and daughter, had not reached that round-house in our relationship where the mother, being old and in need of care, relinquishes authority to the daughter. If Mum refused to reveal secrets, to unload burdens of memory on to my shoulders, then she was in full possession of her faculties; she was dying too young. We were about to miss

a stage of our lives. Since childhood, I'd accepted that there
would be a time when I would take control and look after
my ageing mother. I'd assumed that I would stay on when
the others had left home, keeping Mum company. I'd fore-
seen this time in our lives without a scrap of regret, giving no
consideration to what I might have been missing elsewhere.
There was nothing saintly about it, I wanted it to be that
way.

Now I'd asked a question which had a distinct ring of
finality, and as Mum sat looking back at me, contemplating
her response, I longed to retract it, but it was too late. The
men had already arrived. I couldn't yet see them, of course,
but I felt they were nearby, each one standing stock-still,
waiting like characters in Eliot's *Family Reunion* for the spot-
light to fall on them.

'Oh Eve,' Mum said, her eyes full of mischief, 'I hardly
knew them. Except in the Biblical sense.'

'Never mind, then,' and I waved my hands, hoping to
send the bastards packing.

'No, you should meet them, it's time you did. Get us
both a tot of rum, and then I'll introduce you.'

Rum was my mother's medicine, and her treat. She never
drank soft drinks, it was tea, strong and sweet for her, or
neat rum. We had a glass-fronted cupboard, bowed like a
bay window, where we kept a set of dainty gold-rimmed
glasses and the bottle of rum. We couldn't call it a drinks
cabinet because apart from the rum it contained bric-a-brac
which had nothing to do with imbibing. There was a salt
and pepper set, a pair of blue-birds who'd lost their stop-
pers, and a honey pot shaped like an old beehive, with a
giant, rather grotesque bee balanced indelicately on top.

Junk, all of it. No point, now, in pining for useless trash. But the glasses were pleasing to hold, not cut but smooth as the rum itself, and curved to fit exactly in an open hand. I poured us both a generous amount, taking a good swig of mine for courage, and settled back in my chair.

You might think it was the rum, but once I'd accepted that I was about to meet these legendary men, I was dizzy with excitement. They had been there throughout my childhood, shadowing, walking behind as if playing Grandma's Footsteps. They'd come on visits in the night, filling my dreams, making me strain my ears in case they were downstairs talking to Mum. In every game I played there had been hidden characters, larger than life, but invisible, unmentionable. The Fathers; as elusive and impressive as the God of small children's prayers, often in fact confused with this white-robed powerhouse or with Father Christmas in his red outfit but with the same fluffy facial adornment. Even as a grown-up, clutching a glass of rum, I half expected the appearance of a line of men akin to the seven dwarfs in everything but size.

'The last shall be first, since we're using Bible talk,' Mum knocked back most of her drink in one go and gasped, 'Ahh, right then.'

My heart lost its way and stumbled over beats until I felt my head swim. I was excited, very scared, a little queasy. They were coming, here, now, into this room. The Fathers.

'Samik's dad,' Mum announced. 'There's a sweet man for you.'

I followed the turn of her head in order to see what she saw. Samik's father was conjured to stand in the doorway, a small, narrow silhouette who made me shiver yet stare. His head was round as a football because, I was just able to appreciate, his hair grew straight against his skull, like a tight cap.

'He came down from Greenland, on a fishing boat. Not as interesting to look at as his son, bit on the short side with a flat face. Lovely eyes though, black as jet. He smelt of cod-liver oil and salt, a vast improvement on the beer-and-fags aroma of the local lads. I never could pronounce his real name, so I used to call him Joe, 'cos he was so honest. Naïve too, the green one from Greenland. There, Eve, meet Joe.'

A gentle yellow glow, reminiscent I suspect of old gas lamps, fell on this shadow of a man, touching his clear, olive skin, making his eyes sparkle. I nodded in greeting but got no response. Clearly the vision was one way. I liked the look of Joe. He had a bewildered expression but seemed eager to learn, to please. I knew without enquiring that he'd been a virgin until he fathered Samik. He was young and, as Mum said, sweet. He may have smelt of his trade but he had none of the roughness I associate with men who fish for a living. I smiled at him but he was already starting to fade.

'Bye Joe,' Mum called as if she bumped into him every day. Who knows? Perhaps she did meet him and the others often. I didn't ask. Life has to hold some mystery.

'You liked him,' I said with surprise. Hadn't we always been led to believe that our fathers were great brutes who came, practically raped and plundered, and left a trail of blood, sweat and tears in their wake? But there was Joe, an innocent abroad, and the boot seemed decidedly on the other foot. I'd seen my mum as Victory, tarted to the nines, ready to knock 'em dead, and I knew my own way around the mating game; it wasn't hard to imagine how it had been when Joe's boat docked.

'Course I did. Like I said, a sweet man. What?' she pulled a face at my puzzled, accusing expression, 'You think I should've told him he was a dad? Dragged him back here to support his little boy? Is that it?'

'No, but,' I thought of my brother, how insecure and desperate Samik had been, suffering from the lack of a father. Surely Mum could have allowed him the odd glimpse of Joe? Would that have done any harm?

'I thought it would unsettle the lad,' Mum explained.

I wasn't sure if I'd spoken out loud. Her thought-reading was often confusing.

'Seeing Joe from time to time, like this, and not being able to hug him, to get close, I thought it'd be worse for Samik than not knowing him at all. Call me selfish, but I had my hands full with Django and Merry, I didn't want little Samik becoming seriously disturbed too.'

I nodded, and another sip of rum warmed my throat. My head was developing a pleasing buzz.

'Besides,' there was regret in Mum's voice, but resignation too, 'I could never have let Joe know about Samik. He's a dad several times over now, a grandad too. Such a good man, he'd have found it hard if he'd known, he'd have felt himself pulled two ways.'

I topped up our drinks. I wanted to be seriously tipsy by the time my own old man appeared in the limelight.

'Right, now, Merry's dad,' Mum clicked her fingers and this time the shadow *was* the size of dreams, or nightmares. 'George,' Mum introduced him, 'built like a rock, but with a big heart to match.' Again I was taken aback. Another kind-hearted man. What had happened to the monsters we'd imagined? 'George was a clever bugger, with his hands, he could mend anything. Merry's condition wasn't inherited. George was just a slow mover, deliberate. Liked to think things through before taking action.' The soft light was shining on a face which reminded me of Merry in many ways. Beneath shaggy eyebrows, George's eyes were large, pale and decidedly hangdog. He had a vast beer belly but was otherwise thickset rather than fat. 'A self-taught man, aren't you, George?' Mum smiled. Of course he gave no sign of having heard. 'We were at school together. He was bullied and teased too, left school with nothing, then studied mechanics at home. Runs his own garage now, don't you? Wonderful with engines, but still a little uneasy with his fellow humans. I suppose,' she smiled kindly at our visiting ghost, 'in that respect, you're more like our Django than Merry.'

It occurred to me that Mum might have got muddled, that George *had* fathered Django, not Merry. Although there was a physical resemblance between Merry and this man . . . maybe George had been father to both my unusual brothers? It hadn't struck me before, because Mum never let her men friends hang around, that two or even three of us children might share the same dad. I couldn't cope with the idea of sharing mine, however I might like or dislike him when his turn came. It would have been the same as sharing a security blanket, or letting another child suck your thumb. Mum was busy bidding George goodbye and concentrating on conjuring up a new face. For once she appeared to have no idea what was going on in my head. I tried to steady my racing heart with more rum. Then I realized that Django's father was next in line and George was fading, so I'd been wrong on all counts.

If I'd kept a clear head I'd have known that the man who fathered Django was nothing remotely like George. In a corner of our living room a thin, dark Gypsy appeared. He was less solid, more of a spirit than Joe and George, and infinitely more thrilling. He wore loose cord trousers held by braces over a collarless shirt and his chest, exposed because of missing buttons, was smooth and brown. I can't honestly say he was handsome, although he had high cheekbones and fine eyes, because there was such a look of discontent settled on his face. I knew instinctively that he would have had no interest in me, that women like myself, overweight, pink, would leave him cold. Had I spoken to him, and had he been able to respond, I'd have expected grunts rather than words from his straight, tightly kept lips. Only the exceptional among the fairer sex would loosen that tongue and lighten those eyes, and then only for a short, passionate spell. Apart from the look of discontent, he was the male equivalent of my mother, small, light-boned, agile and busy. I certainly didn't expect Mum to tell me this was a good, kind-hearted man.

'Jake,' she said, 'not as clear as the others on account of our only having met in the dark,' and she laughed warmly, a sound of rum and flirtation. The accompanying smile took years off her face leaving the impression of a girl who was capable of enticing anybody she chose. While Jake was in the room I saw her, young Victory, more clearly than I saw him. She was bright and a little drunk, young but knowledgeable, teasing but deadly serious about having her own way. For once there was no Taff to hang on Victory's sleeve, to giggle out of turn and transform romance into tat; only Victory, dressed in crimson, smelling of violets, smiling, confident, happy.

'He was no angel,' Mum was almost whispering, 'but I came closer to heaven with him than with any man.' And she sent him packing with a clap of her hands, as if his very existence was too much for her.

We had some cheese and biscuits to soak up the rum before I was introduced to Perdita's father. He appeared to have a shine to him that had little to do with the soft lighting. I think it came from his suit. His name was Colin and he'd been a salesman at the time of Perdita's conception. His face made me want to climb from my chair, a movement which would have required quite an effort, and dab him with powder. He seemed uncomfortable with the temperature in the room. In fact the shimmer of sweat on his nose and brow had a permanence that suggested he was unhappy with the temperature of this universe. Standing still was obviously torture to Colin, his hands went from pockets to lapels, up to his damp forelock, back to his pockets, while his legs jigged on the spot. Watching him was making me sweat in sympathy. Having been so excited by the prospect of meeting these men, I was surprised to find myself longing for Colin to vanish again. I believe this must be the effect he has on most people. I'm glad Perdita hasn't met, and will never meet him. I know she imagines herself only one step down from the Royals. Colin left, his shine staying for a couple of seconds after his form had vanished.

'He was just passing through,' Mum explained, giving a short giggle at the innuendo.

We were getting fairly sloshed by this time and apart

from that sinking, apprehensive feeling I had at the prospect of meeting the skeleton from my own cupboard, I was enjoying the evening as much as any I could remember.

Zulema's father was next. A sweetheart of a man, who came, not from India as I'd always imagined, but from South America.

'Mixed blood,' Mum told me, 'half Spanish, half some Indian tribe. Over here to study English, had the dearest accent. Jorge. Another George really, but very different.' Jorge was comfortably round, a man at peace with his body in open sandals and baggy trousers. He was wearing a shirt so white it defied the yellow lighting, and his teeth were bright to match. I found it hard to think of Jorge having sex – and after all he must have done so at least once. It was a little like trying to picture a soft toy with an erection. The rum was definitely doing its evil worst. Still, Jorge didn't seem to mind being mentally undressed, his smile was good-natured, sunny. In fact he was perfect for Zulema, appearing to be conjured from pure sunlight.

When Jorge had gone and Fabian's dad appeared, I gave an involuntary gasp. The man was beautiful. It's rare to meet such beauty head on, even if the handsome face belongs to a ghost. My jaw dropped and I felt myself blush. If this man had been there, in the flesh, I'd have been unable to speak to him. Fabian is good-looking, tall, striking even, but his darker, more streamlined father was a god. Mum laughed at me. 'That was the effect he had on all the girls,' she assured me, 'and best of all, he'd no idea how lovely he was. I rescued him, Sidney's his name by the way, from the clutches of a very undesirable character. I didn't want to spoil him, his innocence was part of his beauty, but somebody had to teach him a few hard facts.'

'Was he musical?' I asked, my voice a hoarse whisper.

'He'd hum a lot, under his breath, but no, he didn't play anything or sing. Maybe Fabe got his talent from me. How about that? I'd have liked to play a guitar or a fiddle.' I was sorry I'd jumped to the wrong conclusion, but I didn't take Mum's suggestion seriously. She knew I credited her with many of the talents her kids had inherited or developed but the only music she played, or had ever seemed to want to play, was on the radio. Whereas Sidney looked incomplete without a violin or a double bass. Maybe he learnt to play later, once he knew his hard facts.

'He can't stay,' Mum told me with mock regret, 'even though he's so easy on the eye. Do you think Fabe would approve, by the way? I meant to ask you that of each of them. Do they live up to expectations? Apart from Colin, that is.'

Before I could answer I found myself getting emotional, losing my voice through the effort to hold back tears. Whether this was true sorrow due to our losses, or fear of the man who was coming next, I'm not sure. I pictured Samik in the arms of Joe, a scene which was followed instantly by one of George bending to greet a tiny Merry. Those two men, at least, met all the requirements of fathers; they were exactly right.

Then it hit me. I'm not a complete fool, Matthew, and it struck me just in time, seconds before my own dream was to come true, that what I was witnessing was nothing more than a conjuring trick. All done by lighting and wish fulfilment. Nothing to do with reality whatsoever. I was seeing what I wanted to see. Had I been absent, and Perdita sitting in my place, Colin would have been so much more the man, upright, intelligent, important, and my father, Eve's dad, would have been a scruffy, insignificant bloke with holes in his shoes.

I looked reproachfully at Mum.

'Had enough?'

I didn't know if she was talking about the rum or this game. Anyway, I was passed caring, having had enough of both. Now that I knew I was less likely to meet my real dad than to fly round the room, I shrugged and told her we might as well make it a full complement.

'My father' appeared in his pool of light, a medium-sized, sandy-haired man, not in any way evil, but not golden with goodness either. Was he the best I could do? This average man with his blue eyes and freckled face?

'What's his name?' I asked with a sigh, knowing the answer a split second before it came.

'David. Dave. Nice enough chap, older than me, kind in his way. What do you think he did for a trade?' she asked, tossing the ball into my court.

'Carpenter I expect.' Another fatherless child's fantasy, having a dad who did the same thing as Jesus' father.

'Spot on.'

But the joy had gone from the evening, from the play-acting, her voice was flat, like my hopes.

Later, in my bed, I wondered if it was for the best. Had I wanted to know each of my mother's secrets? Didn't she have the right, as we all do, to take some of them with her to the grave? That night I was painfully aware that I'd soon be without her, and in my state of dread I was prepared to forgive her anything. Besides, maybe those men were nothing more than dimly remembered shadows to her, ghosts whose shapes and personalities had been altered over the years by the yearnings of her children. She may not have been behaving dishonestly in presenting me with personified dreams; dreams might have been all she herself had to draw on. Also, now that she's gone, I remember The Night Of The Fathers with gratitude and affection. It always used to puzzle me, the way my magic drew the line at managing to tell me anything at all about the fathers. But as the effect of the rum receded and sense returned, I understood that my mother controlled the extent of my powers. That night she'd made an allowance, letting us fuse our magic to conjure those images; a rare and special amalgamation.

My mother took my father with her when she burnt. For all I know that may be a good thing. He could have been a thief or a mass murderer. He may have been nondescript and boring. What good do they do anyway, apart from being handy with a hammer and brave enough to lift spiders from the bath? Some might say I'm lucky, I have an unknown entity that I can mould to fit my needs, a piece of putty to shape into the man who made me. But I don't feel lucky. I long for flesh, no matter how ancient and flabby, to grab in a daughter's hug.

Within days, the trial will be in full swing. I wonder if I'll see a sandy-haired man in the gallery? If so I'm afraid I might burst out laughing. I do want to give a good impression of myself and I know, although I'm not certain I understand why, that frivolity isn't acceptable. Best to keep my eyes down, on my regulation shoes, and my mouth shut except when answering questions. People don't die of being in court, do they? Hundreds go through the courts daily and you hardly ever hear of anybody dying from fright there, from fear of standing or sitting in the judge's line of vision, being Public Enemy Number One.

There's so many questions I ought to be asking. What, for example, is the usual punishment for arson? I don't know if we're talking years or months here, or burning at the stake for that matter. It can't be that bad, I'm sure Mum thought it through, weighing up the options. Presumably she reckoned that I'd suffer less for committing the crime than I would being tied to an empty Cornflake House for the rest of my days. I don't feel reassured, though, I'm not convinced Mum knew what she was asking of me.

Who will come to my rescue? I've asked you not to, and there is nobody else now Mum's dead. My kicking foot has developed into a nervous twitch. I have to walk about in bare feet at night so as not to wake Liz. If I stay in bed my foot rocks both bunks. Her turn is yet to come and I think Liz deserves quiet sleep until then. Quiet sleep, a treat beyond my imaginings . . . but you must go there, I shouldn't be keeping you from sleep. Save me a place under the deep bedcovers.

Twelve

Forgive me for having neglected you for the last few days. Especially when you sent those roses, well the card with roses on which I take to be the next best thing to a real live aromatic bunch. Everything came to a head so fast I hardly had time to wipe my nose, as Mum used to say. Now, as I write this I'm aware, for the first time in days, of the feelings of other people. Liz, for example, has been heading surreptitiously towards a nervous breakdown while maintaining our agreed silence. She probably wouldn't have noticed my kicking foot as she herself is a mass of twitching and jerking. Plus she cries constantly – but without making a sound which excuses me a bit for not having noticed before. Tears drip like water torture down her cheeks and she collects them in her sleeve. I asked her if she'd care to break the habit and talk things over. She shook her head but fell mutely into my arms and soaked my shoulder. The first real hug I've had in ages. Her hair smelt of ash but I don't think she indulges in cigarettes. Maybe this angst is due to a broken love affair with a chain-smoker.

I'm dithering. The truth is that it's hard to begin, especially if I'm to talk not only of what's been going on in court but my reaction to this. I think I said that I might have enjoyed the attention on the night of the fire, had I been a true exhibitionist. Well, I'm not, and walking into court, with all eyes turned on me, I felt exposed and humiliated. I kept my head down, not wanting to see faces familiar or unknown, hoping that I'd become magically invisible. A murmur ran round the room, the rumble of unfriendly thunder. When I did raise my head, I found myself facing the judge, a man. I'd vaguely hoped for a woman, believing a mother or a daughter would have a better understanding of my plight. Mind you, far from being inhuman, the man I found myself staring at was a surprisingly sympathetic looking creature with curly hair and a pink complexion. But his voice, when he told us to sit, *was* impressive and my hands were shaking as they hit my lap. I'll be very critical of films and television shows when they portray the accused casually wandering into court. I don't believe any but the hardened criminal could make that entrance nonchalantly.

There were some awful moments while they sorted out the charge. Inspector Somebodyorother stood with his back to me, as if discussing secrets that should be kept from me. I felt angry and possessive about this, it was my crime after all. Having, only seconds ago, disliked being the focus of attention, I found myself thinking, 'Oy, what about me? I'm the one in the dock here.' I turned offended eyes on Valerie but she was waiting to be called up, to join them, and her gaze was fixed on the inspector's back. She was summoned soon, along with the man heading the prosecution and they huddled around the judge, heads down. I half expected a rugby ball to appear behind them.

The case went public while I was trying to remember the

words to a very rude rugby song that one of Taff's blokes had taught me.

Forensic evidence showed conclusively that my mother hadn't died in the fire. There were enough remains for them to be certain about this, a grisly detail conjuring an image I have tried to block out but which I know will haunt me for ever. There were not enough remains, God can we hurry over this part please, however, for them to say exactly how she *did* die.

'You cannot then rule out the possibility of foul play?' asked the prosecuting counsel. The forensic expert said she couldn't. But then my side, sorry if the terminology has a ring of Cowboys and Indians but at the time it felt a bit like Custer's last stand, my side called some witnesses and saved the day. They called Perdita. I was shocked by this, hearing her trotting in from behind, then seeing her face before me. Who *had* I been expecting? A guardian angel I think. By then I was feeling quite queasy, with memories and nerves, and I'd have liked to be taken out and given a cup of hot, sweet tea instead of having to sit still and listen to Perdita talking about Mum and her illness. She assured Valerie that our mother had indeed been ill, very ill, for some time before her death. Perdita looked as if the BBC had dressed her for the part, young up-and-coming businesswoman, in some courtroom drama. There never was a suit so firm and neatly cut, a blouse so white on a throat so scrubbed. Then, as I mocked, Perdita turned to me and smiled. It was a genuine smile, full of sisterly affection and sympathy. It made the hairs on the back of my neck prickle with guilt. I smiled back but it probably looked as if I was trying not to gag. She frightened me, my little sister to whom I had been a bully rather than a friend. Suddenly she had the power to hurt me, in fact I was hurting very much. I wanted more than anything to be out of that place and free to tell her how sorry I was, not only for making her homeless but for ridiculing her over the years. I wouldn't have felt more restricted if I'd been wearing a ball and chain.

The second witness who confirmed that Mum had been dying was Merry's carer, Jim. He explained how Merry was in the habit of making monthly visits home and how these had grown shorter and more strained as Mum got weaker. Instinctively I searched the court for Merry, expecting to catch sight of him leaping over the jury box or charging at the judge. Without Jim he was sure to run riot. I thought it kind of Jim to come and speak up for me but reckless of him to bring, and then abandon, Merry. Of course the two of them aren't joined at the hip. The Home has other staff. It's just that Jim always accompanies Merry on outings. In my head I must have switched this to 'Merry always accompanies Jim on outings.' This time Merry had been left behind, thank God. I hadn't thought of Jim as anything other than a carer. In court he was an anxious, quietly spoken man who was prepared to help a friend. He'd made an effort for the occasion, his sparse hair was combed out of his eyes and his tattoos were hidden under a pale blue shirt. I was touched by his consideration and tried, in spite of the emotions Perdita had aroused, to give him an appreciative look, but he was nervous and didn't meet my eyes.

The prosecution wanted to know why, if my mother had been ill, no doctor had been involved. They also inferred that the lack of a death certificate was very dubious. Doctors, medicines, bits of paper. Mum hated the lot. Valerie doesn't have the kind of skin that blushes but I could see she was getting hot under the collar at this point. I didn't envy her. I wouldn't have wanted the job of explaining Mum and her quirks to that lot. Having been moved by the support of Perdita and Jim, I tried to distract myself by searching for other familiar faces. Witnesses are kept outside, so that they can appear like white rabbits, but surely if I looked around I'd find a few friendly folk amongst the punters. It took a while, I couldn't turn my head for long, it would've looked rude, but finally I spotted Bing, bless him, sitting with his head down, dreadlocks covering his eyes. I have horribly underestimated my son and my feelings for him. Then more than ever, I wanted to be free, to have time to share with him.

On my next exploration, I saw our next-door neighbour, Mr Lee from Fisher's Close. Not friend but not quite foe. He always was a nosy old fart with no life of his own. I hoped he was enjoying the show, it was the last one he'd have at my expense.

I wasn't running on a full tank (Taff's expression this time) so it took a while for the proceedings to sink in. The judge was gathering papers to his breast, the jury checking their watches.

'There,' Valerie was smiling, 'that's one relief.'

'Not manslaughter?' I guessed, wondering how many reliefs made for an easy mind.

'No, just the charge of arson.'

Right, so I wasn't being accused of killing Mum, only of burning her house to the ground. It sank in, slowly.

Day One was over. I had no clear idea of how things would progress but I felt relieved. A cell is positively cosy compared to a court. I longed for my bunk bed and the almost dark of a prison night. As I was being led from the court a man stepped up and whispered to Valerie who in turn whispered to my warder.

'No,' the warder said, 'I don't think she can have it, not right now. But you can show her it, then give it to her after, if all goes well.' The man, who looked at me like a long lost friend but whose face I didn't recognize, opened his hand. Zulema's moon pendant lay curled on his pink palm.

'I was covered in soot when we last met,' he explained, 'but I'd rescued this from the fire and I didn't know what to do with it.' I couldn't have smiled, any movement of my facial muscles would have brought tears. I stared at the opal until the shape blurred and only white light remained.

'I'll keep it safe for you,' my fireman promised. If I hadn't done so recently, I could have fallen in love on the spot.

I slept well that night. It's the unknown that keeps me awake. Going to court had been my nightmare. Now I knew what to expect the next day, more of the same and not pleasant either. The outcome of the case had paled in comparison to the ordeal of being in the hot seat.

I'd been kidding myself if I thought I knew what was coming. Day Two was far more nerve-racking. For a start I was in the box, being cross-examined by Valerie, knowing the prosecutor was itching to have his turn.

'Would you describe your mother as having been eccentric?' Valerie asked.

'Yes,' I felt like Judas, 'to some she must have seemed that way, but I think of her more as a person who had firmly held beliefs.'

'And it was because of one or several of these beliefs that

you set fire to your family home?' People began to mutter expectantly at this. Although I was pleading guilty to arson, this was to be the first time I'd *admitted* setting fire to my home.

I never had the chance to answer that essential question. There was shouting from beyond the closed doors, a woman's voice yelling about being, or not being, a witness and the firm voice of an official telling her to quieten down. Her refusal to obey was heightened by the way in which the entire court hushed. We could hear her cursing amongst light thuds, presumably as she and the official collided with the doors.

'Evey!' screamed the woman. 'Tell 'em to let me in.'

My heart stopped. I was instantly chilled to the bone. Even through solid doors the Lincolnshire accent was unmistakable. Mum was the only one who called me Evey. My mother had come back from the dead to plead my case. My prayers had been answered. I was practically gagging with joy. I had no doubts, Mum was greater than death, just as she'd always been larger than life. Instinctively I raised my arms for the long embrace.

'Evey!' cried the voice beyond the door. 'Tell 'em.'

'Mum!' I shouted, concentrating on the doors in the hope of opening them from afar. Time raced, whole scenes ran through my head. Mum and I hugging, kissing, promising we'd never part again. The judge smiling, shaking his curly head, banging his mallet to declare the case closed. Valerie looking bewildered as Perdita pushed her way towards us with tears of joy running down her face. All this I experienced in a split second. Then the doors burst open and a round figure stumbled in, tripping and swearing in her hurry to reach the judge. Although it was far from funny to me, I can see now that it was a classic comic entrance. A pair of bandy little legs staggered under the weight of a tree-trunk torso, wide feet squeezed into tight high heels twisted under the strain. As she appeared I let out a cry, the wail of the broken-hearted, of the utterly devastated. You may have heard similar sounds on television, when reporters film women who have lost their children in violent, pointless wars.

My mother hadn't risen from the dead. The combination of the accent and the use of the endearment 'Evey' had tricked me. Air rushed from my lungs as the colour rose in my cheeks. This was magic gone mad, and I was the lady who'd been accidentally sawn in half.

'You got to listen to me,' ordered the flustered new arrival, as the officials made grabs for her and she fended them off with an outsized pink handbag, 'I'm your prime witness.' Another one who'd seen too many TV programmes. I sneaked a look around and saw amazement and amusement on every face, including Perdita's. Even those of us who grew up with Taff are continually taken aback by her being so over the top.

'Madam!' the judge bellowed. 'You are going about this the wrong way. We shall adjourn while you speak to the counsels, then if you have anything of importance to say, you will be given the chance to do so in a civilized manner.' That shut her up, long words always made her gape with wonder.

'The letter,' she hissed at me as she was escorted from the court, 'why the bloody hell didn't you read my letter, Evey?'

'Sorry Taff,' I said to the departing figure. I meant it, I could see she'd come to help me, in her inimitable way, and I needed all the help I could get.

I had to sit in a dingy ante-room while Taff talked to Valerie. I wish I could say that as I sat there I thought kindly of Taff, but the truth is I was horrified by her appearance and still angry with her for not being a reincarnation of Mum. Of all the ironies, this just about took the barrel full of biscuits. I'd prayed for a saviour, begged to be rescued, but by whom? Not for me the loving father, watching from the gallery until his moment came. Oh no. I got my worst enemy, a loud, ludicrous woman, someone I'd never been pleased to see under any circumstances.

To give Taff her due, her appearance had turned my case around, moving me swiftly on from dread to shame. I felt I was trapped in a Whitehall farce or a *Carry On* film. No it was worse than that; it was as if a perfectly good drama had been taken over, halfway through the making, by the director of *Lassie*. When I was led back to find Taff standing in the witness box, looking very pleased with herself, I couldn't help wondering if her great handbag contained a rescue kit, small bottle of brandy, bandages, glucose sweets.

With an effort I reminded myself that this woman had been my mother's best, most constant friend, but I wasn't much comforted by that. Now she was my confederate, I assumed, an ally in my camp. I wasn't greatly comforted by this either. I believe I gave an audible sigh as I sat down. Valerie looked at me as if I'd belched loudly. Then she crossed the floor and began to question Taff.

It was hard for Taff to restrain herself. She wanted to blurt out her story in one breath but Valerie kept her on a tight reign and guided her until it seemed almost as if we were listening to a sane, ordinary person. Throughout the opening questions my mind wandered around in a daze and I thought of other visitations I'd suffered from this witness. I remembered one time when Taff had arrived on the back of a motorbike, her hair knotted round her face, her body encased in red leather. What a sight. Taff has never been slim, her womanly curves may have attracted men in her youth but they spread to Humpty-Dumpty proportions by middle age. All right, I'm not slender myself, but then I'd not be seen dead in tight red skins, motorbike or no motorbike. Her companion, a man half her age glorying in the name of Shane, had a matching set of leathers in bright blue.

'We had to make do with red for Taff,' he told us regretfully, 'because they don't do these in pink.' This comment was the final straw. I had to be taken away by a kindly Zulema as I snorted with hopeless laughter. The idea of Taff trussed up in pink leathers, looking naked but fit to burst any moment, was too much.

Then there was the time she brought a poodle with her. Maybe she was beginning to lose her charms, the poodle appeared to be instead of a man. It was an unhappy dog, with eyes that collected clumps of brown sleep. She carried it about under her arm.

'Is that a child substitute?' Mum asked, for once speaking just a little harshly.

'No, it's a fucking poodle,' and Taff laughed until her smoker's cough turned to a choking fit.

'Well then put it down and let it walk,' Mum ordered. The dog was lowered to the floor where it was instantly attacked by our own mutts. As I've said, we were never cruel to animals. Perdita grabbed the poodle, disentangling him from the jaws of our dogs and was given, for her pains, the job of looking after the little visitor for the duration. I think the thing she minded most, as she carried the poor soul around, was his scruffiness. Taff, having only just acquired him, hadn't had time to take him to a parlour and have him clipped down and puffed up.

Then, another time . . . I was brought sharply back to the present by hearing my name. Not only my name but the endearment which had previously been Mum's prerogative.

'Tell 'em where the letter is, Evey,' Taff was begging. 'What've you done with that letter I sent?' For a while, as she gave me her most pleading look, I wondered what the hell she meant. Then the scent of violets drifted in my direction and I knew Mum was prompting me to concentrate harder – because Taff had been sent to help me.

'The letter,' I muttered while Taff gave me encouraging nods. The unopened post. Yes, I remembered, it was in my cell, lying under your frog. I was allowed, with my warder, to leave the court and search for this missive. Of course I knew where it was, but I didn't want anybody else to touch the frog. The letter was found and we marched back to court. It was not unlike a historical scene, with the King's pardon arriving seconds before the executioner raises his axe. I knew that sealed envelope contained information which would save me. My magic was returning. I honestly felt the air about my head clear. It was rather like having my ears syringed. There was a spell of painful but exquisite tingling noises and a low hum, then a popping sound and Hey Presto. After that I found myself smiling, a kid with the present she most wanted. I smiled at Taff as I was led past her, I gave Valerie a grin, I even beamed at the judge. Only Taff smiled back, flashing her undoubtedly false teeth.

There was a hubbub in court, like actors saying 'rhubarb, rhubarb,' and I knew that if I wanted, I could have picked out one mutter from the far back and isolated it in order to listen in. Magic is exhilarating, even when you choose not to use it. I'd missed being special, missed knowing I could interfere with the normal, make the world a more interesting place. I was so pleased with myself that it took a nudge from Valerie to make me pay attention to what was happening. My letter had been opened and the judge was reading through it. I thought of Taff's language and blushed, but when I looked across at my mother's friend she was nodding her head at the judge, silently agreeing with what he was reading.

'Hope the language isn't too blue,' I whispered to Valerie and I inclined my head in Taff's direction, 'she's famous for her swearing.'

Valerie put her mouth to my ear, 'You haven't been taking any of this in, have you?' she hissed. 'That letter's not from the witness, well there is an enclosed note from her to you, but the essential part, the evidence we need, is from your mother.'

I gripped her arm so hard I imagine I left my mark, 'Say that again.'

'It's a letter from your mother to Mrs Davenport.'

'Who?' I'd forgotten that Taff had once married a man called Davenport; she'd divorced him so fast you'd think his name would've gone with him.

'From your mother to the witness,' Valerie's patience was running out.

'From my mother . . .'

'Yes. Written several weeks before her death.'

To give myself time to recover, I gazed at the judge. He had put on a pair of specs but even so he was squinting at the page of notepaper. Not smart, blue Basildon Bond like you use, Matthew. This was from Mum all right. The thin, white, lined paper he was holding took me straight back to The Cornflake House. My heart ached to see it. And on this familiar paper would be my mother's writing. The judge wasn't squinting because the writing was small, but because it was ill formed. She was no great writer, Mum. I could hardly remember having seen her handwriting, she was adept at getting one of us kids to jot things down for her.

'My hands are floury, Eve,' she'd say, or, 'I'm all wet, Dear, write a message to Fabe for me will you?'

I wonder if she went to the pantry first, and covered her hands in flour, or if she purposefully began the washing-up every time a note needed writing.

'You say it's written from Mum to Taff, not to me?' I asked Valerie.

She shook her head, laying a sympathetic hand on mine, 'But it contains information which will clarify your mother's wishes, do you see?'

Yes, I did. The thin paper collapsed the moment the judge stopped supporting it with his spare hand. Cheap stuff. Trees pulped to tissue. Lines to guide the unsteady hand. No need to wonder why Mum hadn't asked me to write that letter for her, it contained secrets. Secrets she'd struggled to keep, straining to put pen to paper in spite of her problem with words and her illness. I was upset by this, wishing she'd written to me, left a message for me, until I realized that she knew I'd have burnt any such letter along with everything else.

Mum's letter to Taff proved once and for all that I had set fire to The Cornflake House at her bidding. '*I have asked Eve to burn the house down the moment I'm dead,*' it said, as plain as that. This has thrown a new light on my case, a glimmer of hope. It isn't enough to clear me, the case has been adjourned for two days.

During this respite I'm not allowed visitors, so I shall make do with sobbing Liz and with your card. Having my magic back I've lost the doubts that haunted me. I *know* the roses on the card are substitutes for the real thing. I can sense the emotions you were feeling when you wrote your message. By running my fingers over your handwriting I can feel that you wrote the word 'love' with trepidation, but that you meant it. Scary, isn't it? What can I say to calm and reassure you? You are my shooting-star wish come true. I will never let you down. I will be there for you as long as that's what you want. Now I understand the frog too, it was symbolic, wasn't it? Even the colour was no coincidence. Are you green when it comes to love, Matthew? I find that hard to credit, since you are the most desirable man in the world to me. Never mind, I'm practised in the art, and after all, I did train as a teacher.

The return of my magic has enabled me to look at this gift anew. Perhaps magic consists largely of the ability to absorb information not only about myself but about anybody I single out. Is that magic, or merely common sense? I shall sleep tonight, and dream not of fathers but of lovers, of a frog who turns into a prince when the imprisoned princess places her lips on his.

Having spent the worst two days of my life waiting, I was led back to court this morning. It was a clearer case for the judge and jury, but if Mum thought she'd free me by writing to Taff, she was wrong. Taking into consideration the time I've already served, I'm to be moved to the Midlands to spend a further three months at Her Majesty's pleasure. 'Ooh goody,' said the queen of my imagination, 'that fat blonde girl's got another three months porridge.' The judge told me that no matter how much I loved my mother and wanted to obey her wishes, he could not condone my actions. It seems that, as adults, we have to make choices and the right choices have nothing to do with family love or duty, because they must always fall within the law.

Valerie seemed pleased with my sentence but then she doesn't have to start over in a new prison, laying down ground rules with a fresh cell mate and fighting off another load of bullies. They can have my biscuits this time. I shall emerge in three months, thinner and unscarred. Until then I don't want you to see me. Forgive me if this sounds harsh. I need this extra time to myself and I think you do too. I want you to meet as many women as possible while I'm away. Draw comparisons, I shan't be offended. I think I've awakened in you an understanding that you may be attractive. This being a novel concept, you might now be wondering if you could have done better for yourself. You do love me, Matthew. You just don't know if you love *only* me, yet.

They're coming to take me away. See you in three months.

Thirteen

Thanks for your letter, Matthew. I can't repent and let you visit, the three months apart has become part of the process of healing for me. I need to hurt before I can fully enjoy. But believe me I'm delighted to hear that you're missing me. Not falling into the arms of another woman yet? I'm astonished to find you haven't been snapped up, but then I'm biased. Of course I'd know if you had found a new love; the magic has stayed, making my life in this hell-hole a lot easier. The other prisoners don't bother me. I walk in peace, surrounded by an invisible iron curtain. Big Bad Eve, don't mess with her. Sometimes it seems I've been inside so long I shan't know how to be free; freedom is a lesson I'll need to learn from scratch. I've taken on a prison persona, a tough, abrupt woman of whom I've grown quite fond. She and I shall have to say goodbye in a month's time. One month, surely you can wait 'til then?

I have had one persistent visitor here. She won't leave me alone, although at first I refused to see her, sending messages to say I was ill or busy. I am busy, funnily enough. I've been given the task of rearranging the library. Not simply A-Z, but sub-divisions in the existing categories. Now fiction is split into Romance, Thrillers, Sci-Fi etc. It's made me realize how much reading I've yet to do, so many authors, so little time. Since I stopped writing to you, I read until my eyes ache, until they turn out the lights, but I'll never catch up with myself. And I've made a new friend, well two actually. I said I'd try this out, friendship, and I rather like it.

I share a cell with a woman called Maggie who is so ordinary that at first it was hard to think of her as anything other than a housewife who had popped in for a chat. She is middle-aged, has a kind, honest face, a Birmingham accent and hair which is growing out from a fairly disastrous perm. Our conversation centres around ideal ways of cleaning sinks and how to get stains out of T-shirts. Not my specialist subjects, but Maggie has knowledge enough for two. For days, assuming she was simply missing her kitchen and her pile of washing, I humoured her, nodding when she recommended this soap powder over that, playing interested. Then I discovered that she's in here for stabbing her husband eight times with a carving knife and that the T-shirt and sink in question had been haunting her since the night she tried in vain to wash pints of blood out of one and down the other. Suddenly I wasn't *playing* interested any more. Sadly Maggie has blanked all but the washing from her memory and can tell me no more about her night of crime. I don't even know how the husband fared; neither, it seems, does she. Frustrating, isn't it? Was the man a complete bastard, making her life a misery for years on end? Or did he play around, meaning to leave his homely wife for a younger, more attractive woman? Maybe neither, perhaps Maggie just flipped from boredom, finding herself tied to the kitchen one day too long. We'll probably never know. Maggie is stuck at her sink, in her imagination, a modern Lady Macbeth, endlessly trying different cleaning products.

My other friend is the librarian, Stella. True to her name, she's a real star. Stella treats me with unqualified respect, not showing a scrap of interest in my crimes but being genuinely enthusiastic about my background.

'Can't waste skills like yours,' she insisted and set me straight to my task. For hours on end we work side by side, passing each other with arms full of books, absorbed in searching, filing, checking. Prisoners come and go but I hardly see them. What I do envisage is the impression their choice of book will make on them. I'm not talking of reform, simply of the marvellous impact of reading. A book adds to a person. When they reach the end, readers have expanded themselves. Take two women, criminals say, shut up here for a couple of years. Then take a novel, let's choose *Oliver Twist* in this instance. One woman reads Dicken's poignant work, the other doesn't. The reader will leave with more, will go away having had a relationship with Nancy, Bill and Fagin; she'll be greater by the sum of that book. Also she will have joined the club, the band of those who know this work. Do you see? As I said, so many books . . . It was easy to convince myself that I was too busy reading and growing to see my visitor.

But this was no ordinary caller, not one to be fobbed off, never one to take no for an answer. She came repeatedly, leaving little calling cards, notes scribbled on the back of bus tickets, written on the inside of chocolate wrappers. 'See me,' they pleaded. There was one worked painstakingly between the lines of a telephone bill. She must have picked

this bill up on the bus to the prison, I suppose, where it had
been dropped by another visitor. This is how it reads:

Breakdown of information
'Don't try and avoid me, Evey,'
Summary of call charges
'I only want a chat after all,'
Total call charges £67.94
'I come a long way'
Family & Friends
'and I need to sit and talk.'

As I studied it I had this vision of her on the bus, anxious,
eager. An elderly woman making a difficult journey, riding
that route taken only by family and foolhardy but firm
friends of the incarcerated. I was still shocked by another,
clearer message I'd had from her, one written on thin, white,
lined paper. Shocked doesn't do my feelings justice. Infuri-
ated comes closer, or staggered. But the telephone bill was
a missive straight from the land of childhood, taking me
back to the muddle, the absurdities of The Cornflake House
which is where, despite everything, I have wanted to be all
this time. I couldn't refuse to see her any longer. My visitor
had every right to ride that bus along with those other long
suffering relations. It was my mother, you see, pestering,
begging, longing just to see me.

My mother. It takes a bit of getting used to, I can tell you.
Such an emotive word, that and its companions, mothered,
motherless. I'd begun to get used to motherless, now I have
to adjust to the likelihood of being mothered again. Loved
in that unique way, as I love Bing. I have no mother. I have

a mother. Very little difference, on paper; but away from the page, everything is changed.

The woman simply will not leave me alone. Burning The Cornflake House was supposed to liberate me, to free me for the remainder of my life and to release Mum's spirit. Instead I'm a prisoner, physically constricted and mentally trapped in a web of family which even my own death wouldn't unravel.

I mentioned the letter, didn't I? The one that preceded the scribbled notes? I'll copy the letter out for you. It's a classic, a schoolteacher's nightmare:

'Darling Girl,

You must be wandering why you was asked to burn down your house,' she wrote, 'and now you must be feeling cross' (cross!) 'because you've landed up inside. Don't blame her, Evey, there was things inside The Cornflake House should never have been kept, but Vic was like that, kept every bloody thing, specially papers cos she thought these should be kept when others would have throwed them out.'

It rambled on in this vein and I almost gave up on it. Almost. Now I wish I had chucked it in the bin unread. Not that I'd have escaped. As I said, the writer was intent on being either seen or heard. To continue:

'These papers that got burnt I suppose along with your clothes and stuff told to many secrets, I'm not saying Vic wasn't a true Gypsy and wanted to go that way and take it all with her, but most important was those papers. They had to go. Do you see, Lovey? Are you following? It was all written down and stuffed in a box somewhere then knowing Vic it got lost, about your Dads, the truth about them and about your Mum as well. Not one of you was her own flesh and blood. I can't keep quite any more.

Maybe Ill be sorry, but my days are numberd and I have to have my say. Sorry to shock you Sweetheart, but Vics gone, God bless her, and I kept shut up to long.'

Are you following, Matthew? Can you love a woman who's been duped right through her life? Can you love the bastard child of an old tart like Taff? More importantly, can I love myself, or at least learn to *like* being who I am? The letter went on to explain, gushingly, how Taff had given birth to me in a place far from home. But being 'a flighty soul' she hadn't felt able to give me the love I deserved. Victory, on the other hand, wasn't flighty, didn't even like male company, and therefore, not being driven by similar urges, was happy to take on the role of mother. So happy that she offered this service not once, but seven times. We Cornflake House kids were as good as orphans, seven souls without a proper parent between us.

I was shaken at first. Mum was not Mum, but Taff was. It look hours to sink in. Then I was embarrassed for having been simple-minded. I was eight when Samik was 'born'. I didn't know the facts of life in detail but I understood that babies came from a mother's stomach. Shouldn't I have noticed the flatness of Victory's tummy? I suspect her of trickery. She must have been capable of puffing herself up. I can't have been the only one who was fooled. After this I grew angry. Secrets are all very well, but we are talking basic human rights here. A child should know its parents, or at the very least, its parent. Neither Victory nor Taff had any right to leave me in the dark so long. I'm in no fit state to receive a shock of this magnitude now, either. How dare they? I hated them both for a while, and Grandma Editha who must have known too. What fun they must've had, all in on the act, cosy together. I wished I had a kitchen of my own, I was in just the right mood for smashing some china. Beyond anger was a void, numb surprise; back to being staggered, in fact.

I couldn't believe that during our formative years, while we were dreaming of and searching for our fathers, we children should also have been looking out for our mothers. No .wonder Victory could only conjure phantom men for me that night, she probably never even met our dads. Perhaps when I eventually capitulated, walked to the Visitors' Room and sat opposite Taff, it was because at least she really did know who's sperm had made me. Except, in retrospect, having been flighty and given to urges, she's not a reliable informant either.

Well, I've seen Taff several times since reading that letter, very awkward meetings at first, with her weeping into a pile of Kleenex and me studying her wrinkled brow for family likenesses. It is from her that I get my fair hair and my tendency to put on weight. It seems my dad was a dark, handsome hunk; but then she would say that. Taff's been with some pretty horrendous men and I've yet to hear her admit that any of them were less than perfect. Please God I haven't inherited her lack of taste. At night I lie awake imagining my future self in a home full of orange glass ornaments and plastic flowers. During these bedtime stories, as I grow older, I begin to resemble Taff in every way, getting fatter, coarser, more eccentric, until, having also inherited her sense of humour, I can see the funny side of the situation. My inheritance isn't a home or possessions, it is Taff. If I couldn't be Victory's daughter, I might have been anybody's;

but I'm not. I'm the flesh and blood of the woman I've spent my life loathing; of the woman my 'mother' loved best.

I, who mourned the loss of my mother deeply, have been given a second chance. Isn't that what bereaved folk long for? You lose a mother, you want a mother; it's every mother-less child's dream.

It was during my second meeting with Taff that a blinding thought occurred to me. I hardly dared to ask, not sure which would be most alarming, an answer of yes, or a disturbing no. She was chatting away at the time, telling me how she'd got something for me, how she hoped the size was right. I wasn't paying much attention, my mind being occupied by my blinding thought.

'Here you go, Lovey,' she said and passed a Tesco's carrier bag across the table to me. I put my hand inside before looking. The contents were soft as candyfloss, but without the stickiness. When I pulled the gift out it was actually the colour of candyfloss but garnished with a bright orange. Three knitted tubes, joined at the shoulders by thick blue thread.

'It's a woolly,' Taff told me. I was grateful for this infor-mation.

'You made it?' A fairly safe guess.

'Just,' she grinned. My blinding thought was momentarily banished to a dark corner as I pictured her in the Home, knitting furiously into the night so as to have this thing ready to present to me on time.

'Thanks,' I offered as graciously as I could. 'Taff?' I hadn't yet managed to call her mother, and the name Mum was taken, but since her revelation I used the name Taff awkwardly. She waited. 'I've just had a thought. Maybe it's absurd but I have to ask. You say that you're my mother . . .'

'I am, I am,' she cried and many heads twisted to look at her earnest expression.

'Yes. Well, I was wondering if that was it, surprise-wise, or if there's more you'd like to tell me?'

The woman blushed deeply, turning her thick make-up from suntan to sunset. She played with the Tesco bag, twisting a corner into a horn.

'Please,' I prompted, 'I need to know.' For a second I thought she was going to begin an I-don't-know-what-you-mean routine, she looked coy enough to do so. She's no coward though. Leaving the bag alone, looking me straight in the eye, she told me I was a smart one and no mistake. At this I picked up the sweater and crumpled it in my hands, holding it under my chin like a security blanket. It would be taken off me when the visit was over, for a while, kept back. It made my skin itch anyway.

'So I'm right?' I whispered.

'No use denying it now,' she admitted. Some might have expected her to look a little ashamed of herself, or at least to pretend to be abashed. I knew her better than that; the pride on her face was no surprise to me.

'All of us?' I marvelled.

She nodded, 'Every last one.'

The answer, being yes, seemed both better and more upsetting than a no might have been. Yes, she had given birth to each one of us kids. This meant that I still had a family, people other than Taff were flesh of my flesh, which was, as Oscar Wilde would have said, a good thing. It had been lonely out there, in the wasteland of only-childness, but now I could return to cosy shared bedrooms, big family meals, the joys of being a family member. On the other hand, Taff's yes meant that I'd been carried in the womb of a monster. The woman had left not only me but Fabian, Zulema, Perdita, Merry, Django (well . . .) and Samik (how could a mother leave Samik?) to be brought up by her best friend. Then, while Victory mothered us, she'd popped in and out of our lives, like an auntie, or a granny or, it has to be said, just as a lot of fathers do.

I studied her, sitting opposite me, and saw no resemblance to any of my brothers and sisters. Just my luck to have been the only one to inherit her colouring and her bulk.

This, Revelation Number Two, puts me in a tight spot. Do I tell my siblings the ghastly truth, or let them live in blissful ignorance? Maybe I should inform the strong and fool the weak. Perdita would probably keel over if she knew, not from shock but from mortification. Fabe, I think, will find it hilarious, I can hear him laughing now and crying, 'No way. Taff? No way.' Merry and Django are unlikely to take any of it in; Merry isn't capable of understanding and Django wouldn't allow himself to absorb information which could unbalance his precarious status quo. What about Samik? This might be too confusing for him to grasp. On the plus side, it might finally drive him from the safe but dull arms of Margaret. My God, to think of Margaret with this new mother-in-law; it almost makes the whole mess worthwhile. Taff might also, perhaps, be able to provide him with that long-lost father he so craves. I think I'll make a deal with myself, I'll only tell Samik on the condition that along with this new, alarming mother, comes a father to complete the set.

That leaves Zulema. I shall have to tell her, to stay silent would be cruel. Besides, I have to share my feelings with somebody close. Not having seen her since Mum, or should I now say Victory?, died has been agony for me. I miss Zulema every day. Maybe this news will persuade her from her hideaway, back to the real world of people as diverse as me and Bing and Taff.

It's not easy having two Mums. I feel a traitor if I so much as think of Taff as 'Mum', because no matter what, I can't abandon Victory, can't dislike her, let alone desert her. She may not have given me life, but she saw to it that I had a life worth living. There was never a time when I felt, as many natural children must, that my mother didn't love me. Victory's love was all-encompassing and unconditional. If you need proof of that you only have to look at Merry and Django. People joke about 'sending them back' when children are difficult or different. Victory probably could have done this, if she'd been less of a mother.

I feel such a fool. There I was, filling pages with what I considered to be essential information about myself, telling you stories to express my love for my mother, to help you appreciate the real me, when I was not that woman's daughter in the first place. Who or what are we? We must be more than seeds surely, more than chemical infusions. I came, not from a magical, marvellous young woman called Victory, but from Taff. Cut me to the bone and find 'made in Taff' printed there in sticky peppermint. In this farce, it's my turn to lose my trousers.

There are a million questions I need to ask Taff. She knows this and the knowledge gives her confidence. I'll have to go on seeing her until every one is answered. There is the issue of whose issue each of us is, if you see what I mean. The father question rears its fascinating head yet again. Where are they now? Which ones are alive and which have passed away? I doubt if Taff has kept in touch with these seven special men, there having been a fan club as long as your arm in her life. Once her relationships ended, we never clapped eyes on the old loves again. But to meet them, it's still a dream that won't end. I didn't find the courage to ask, when gleaning details about my dad, whether he is still with us. Only part of me wants to know.

One question I have posed was about the magic. It puzzled me because I'd assumed it was inherited, passed down through the genes.

'A gift,' Taff told me, 'like that Sleeping Beauty story when the fairy godmothers came to the christening. Not that you were christened, like the princess was, though I'd have liked to be godmother myself, but Vic gave you and Zulema sort of christening prezzies anyway. She said she could tell you two wouldn't confuse them.'

'You mean abuse,' I said.

'Yes,' the smile she gave me was permeated with affection, 'you always were a clever girl.'

Here is yet more proof that Victory pulled all the strings. Had my powers equalled Mum's, I would have felt in my bones that Taff was more to us children than unrelated 'aunt'. As it was, I never suspected; I was never meant to. It was a measured dose of magic Victory bestowed on her two most reliable daughters.

Odd, isn't it? While I was fretting because I thought Victory might love Taff more than she loved me, Victory was probably worrying that I'd form a bond with my natural mother. Maybe I did sense something, and that was why I felt such antagonism towards Taff. Hate and love, two sides of the same coin, they say.

What the hell, Matthew, Taff's a mess, but she's warm-hearted. She's devoted to me, and she's alive. More than alive, full of life. And she is a constant; a vital link with my past. But she's not exactly young, she may not be around much longer. I don't fancy years of feeling guilty for having spurned her. I reckon I should give her a chance.

When I get out of here I'm going to learn freedom; to discover how to eat decent food again, how to get drunk, how to live a little and love a lot. I'll begin by taking you, Bing and 'my mum' out for a slap-up meal: five courses and silver-wrapped chocolate mints with the coffee.